RESISTING RORY

THE DONOVANS
BOOK TWO

SASSA DANIELS
DANIELLE GILLIS

Edited by
MARIA HEARN

CHAPTER ONE

Eleanor

THEY SAY if you lie down with dogs, you get fleas. I can't help but think there's some truth to that. I feel slightly grubby, as if I've done something wrong. Although the club looks great, and people are enjoying themselves, I wonder if I made a mistake in accepting work from Andrew Donovan.

He may masquerade as a respectable businessman, but everyone knows his family heads up one of the most ruthless criminal organizations in the country. I hesitate to use the word Mafia, but that's exactly what they are. It bothers me to think I'm playing a part, however small, in making them richer. What sort of person does accepting money from them make me?

The club is the second I've designed for Andrew. The first was in the basement of one of his family's luxury hotels, another front for their illegal activities. I was called in to finish the job after the previous designer let him down.

It was actually Andrew's wife, Libby, who reached out to me. We were at school together. I thought she was doing me a favor, throwing a prestigious design project my way, but now I'm not so sure.

Her husband has me working on a third nightclub remodel for him, and I'm starting to wonder if I'll ever get the chance to do other projects. Once you're involved with people like the Donovans, it's hard to find a way out.

I didn't want to come here tonight. The less time I spend around the family, the better. But it's the grand opening and it would have looked odd if the person responsible for the interior design didn't attend. Appearances matter to the Donovans. It's why they work so hard to make themselves look respectable.

From the moment I stepped through the door, I've felt uncomfortable. I'm experiencing the sensation that comes from being watched. I don't like it. As I look out over the bustling dance floor from the VIP section, a shiver lifts my shoulders and sets them back down again. Goosebumps form on my skin, and I get a sense of what it's like to be in a predator's sights.

Knowing exactly whose eyes are on me, I don't dare turn around. To do so would be as good as inviting him to join me. I know how Rory Donovan operates. If he sees an opening, he'll take it. I have to keep him at arm's length. Rory can be quite charming when he wants to be but, like the rest of his family, he's dangerous.

After a while, I realize I can't stand here staring out over the dance floor all nigh, so I turn and immediately meet Rory's gaze. I guess I was right about him watching me, but I don't understand why he's paying me so much attention. Although we flirted a bit at Libby and Andrew's wedding last year, I turned him down when he wanted to go somewhere more private. I thought my rejection would out him off. If anything, I think it made him more interested in me.

He's standing by the bar on the opposite side of the room with his older brother, Aidan, who's head of their family. The two men are engaged in conversation, but Rory's focus seems to be very much on me.

Under such intense scrutiny, I don't know what to do with myself. My instinct is to flee, but the last thing I want is to give a seasoned hunter an excuse to chase me. He's the type of man who'd get off on catching me and dragging me back to his bed. I just wish that thought didn't make my insides tingle.

Now that I've met his gaze, it's hard to look away from Rory. There's something magnetic about the man. He exudes power and confidence. He's pretty easy on the eyes, too. Tall and broad-shouldered, he fills out his expensive navy suit well. His shirt is slightly stretched across his chest, giving the impression of a muscular torso beneath. His dark hair is tousled, like he just rolled out of bed. Maybe he did. Who knows?

His eyes are a deep, chestnut brown. From this distance, I can't see it, but there's usually a wicked gleam in them. It's been a struggle to resist the temptation to play with this bad boy, but I'm aware I'd be out of my depth with someone like him. I don't understand the rules of his world. I've only ever dated nice, safe men.

Just as the staring contest between us gets really awkward, I catch movement in the corner of my eye. I let out a breath of relief as Libby heads toward me. Though we weren't friends at school, we get on well now, and I'm glad she's here to act as a distraction from Rory's intimidating presence. Her husband is with her, gripping her hand tightly. He probably doesn't want to let her out of his sight. From what I've seen, Andrew is the possessive type.

"This place looks amazing." Libby throws her arms around me and pulls me in for a hug. "Andrew told me it was even better than the last job you did, but I didn't think that was possible."

"Thanks," I mutter as I disentangle myself from her embrace. My cheeks are heated, the result of being on the receiving end of praise I don't deserve. Though I am pleased with the abstract floral design on the walls and I love the plum-colored sofas in the VIP lounge, there's nothing ground-breaking in my design. Every time someone compliments me on it, my imposter syndrome flares up.

"Let's grab a seat."

As with every suggestion Andrew makes, I get the feeling compliance is not optional. I follow him and his wife to a quiet booth in the corner, admiring Libby's silver sequined mini-dress. It's amazing, clinging to her curves and falling just a few inches beneath her butt, to show off her stunning legs. I have no clue how she's managing to walk so confidently in her towering heels, but she makes it look easy.

In comparison, I must appear frumpy in my knee-length black dress, which is really more suitable for office wear. I did actually buy it a couple of years ago for a job interview at a design consultancy before I decided to try my luck at freelancing.

I knew the dress wasn't suitable for a nightclub, but I wanted to maintain an air of professionalism tonight, especially since I knew Rory would be here. I hoped my plain dress, matched with distinctly unsexy ballet flats, would persuade him I'm too staid for a man of the world like him and he'd look elsewhere for amusement. So far, it doesn't seem to be working. I can feel his eyes following me across the room.

Libby slides onto one of the seats in the booth and Andrew gets in next to her, his massive frame creating an effective barrier between her and anyone who might want to do her harm. It also blocks her from other men's views, which I'm sure for him is an added bonus. I sit opposite them, dropping my purse onto the seat next to me.

Andrew gestures subtly, raising a single finger to get the attention of one of the waitresses. Mere moments later, the young blonde woman scurries over with a bottle of champagne and three glasses. It must be nice to have the power to command people like that, to have them anticipate your every need.

"Leave the bottle, Stella," Andrew says.

It doesn't surprise me he knows her name. From experience, I get that he's very hands on with his businesses. He seems to be familiar with the lives of everyone who works for him.

"So how is the Soho project coming along?" he asks as he pours three glasses of champagne.

"It's on track to open at the end of the month." Thankfully, everything is running smoothly. The major structural work has been done, and it's time to install the kitchen, the restrooms and the bar, as well as sorting out the finer details of the décor.

"Good. I have another project for you."

My heart sinks. I've been afraid of this. I try not to let my trepidation show.

"Oh, what is it?"

"A restaurant in Piccadilly. It's got a Mediterranean theme right now, but I want to turn it into an Irish pub, something with a very traditional vibe."

That could be a lot of fun, but I still wish I could turn him down. A believable excuse for why I can't take on the project doesn't spring to mind, so I nod.

"Okay, so what's the timeframe?"

Andrew lifts a shoulder in an indolent shrug. "I want to be up and running as soon as possible, but you'll need to look the place over and let me know how long you think it'll take."

"I'll get onto it as soon as I can."

"Good."

Andrew hands Libby a glass of champagne and slides another across the table to me. He raises his own glass and Libby and I both mirror him.

"To another successfully completed project," he says, gesturing around the packed club, "and many more to come."

Inwardly shuddering at that thought, I clink my glass

against each of theirs, then take a sip of the cool, crisp champagne. Andrew gets to his feet.

"I'll leave you ladies to catch up."

He walks off to greet his brothers at the bar. They've now been joined by their sister-in-law, Sorcha. The only one missing is Jacob, the nicest of the bunch from what I've seen.

I can't help feeling sorry for Sorcha as I watch her standing there with those men. It's not just because she was widowed so young. Since her husband, Ciaran, the former head of the family, died, she's had his four over-protective siblings watching everything she does.

Being under Andrew's scrutiny at work, or Rory's on the rare occasion we're in the same place, annoys me. I can't imagine what it's like to be stuck in a gilded cage like Sorcha, or Libby, for that matter.

"It's Andrew's birthday next week," Libby says. "We're having a small dinner party, just family and friends."

I hope she's not about to invite me. Being involved with the family professionally is bad enough. I don't want to get entangled in their personal lives, no matter how much I like Libby.

"Do you want me to make the cake?" I ask.

I somehow ended up making their wedding cake since they got married at short notice, so fingers crossed that's what she was going to ask.

"No, that's taken care of." She puts her glass down on the table and leans forward. "I want you to come to the dinner."

"Oh, uhm, I don't know. I'm really busy."

Libby's face falls. "You can spare one night, surely?"

"I don't know. Like I said, I have a lot on."

"Yeah, I appreciate that. It's just, well, I don't have a lot of friends apart from you. Most people turned their backs pretty quick after my mum died."

Her mother was shot dead in the street by mobsters looking for her father. I don't know the whole story, but I believe Edward Preston got into trouble with the Russian Mafia and they killed his wife to teach him a lesson. The people who once clamored to be Libby's friend shunned her in the wake of the scandal.

"I know, and I'd love to come and spend celebrate Andrew's birthday with you. It's just…"

"Rory?" Libby guesses. "Has he done something?"

I shake my head because, in fact, he hasn't really done anything. He's let me know he wants to fuck me and he watches me intently, but he's not tried to pressure me in any way.

"No, but I find him a little intense."

Libby laughs. "He can be, but once he's had a couple of glasses of wine and some birthday cake, he'll be a pussycat."

I don't bother pointing out that unless she plans to serve the cake first, that's not going to help me get through dinner with him.

"Okay, I don't suppose it will hurt to take a night off."

"Great!" Libby's face lights up, making me glad I relented. "It's Thursday at 8."

"Should I bring anything? What about a gift?"

Panic seizes hold of me at the thought of trying to find the perfect present for a wealthy mobster who's also kind of my boss at the moment.

"Oh, don't worry about that." Libby waves a hand dismissively. "Andrew won't expect anything."

"Maybe not, but I hate to turn up empty-handed."

"Well, he likes malt whisky and you wouldn't know it to look at him, but the man's a chocoholic."

"Really?"

"Oh yeah, you can't go wrong with chocolate."

I doubt an ordinary chocolate bar is going to cut it, but at least Libby's given me something to work with.

As Andrew saunters back over to us, I decide to make my excuses and leave.

"I'm going to call it a night," I say as I shuffle along my seat and get to my feet.

"It's only eleven thirty," Libby protests.

"I know, but I'm tired. It's been a long day."

"Not working you too hard, am I?" Andrew asks. To his credit, he does manage to inject some concern into his tone. "You need to take some time off."

"She's coming to your birthday dinner next week," Libby says

"Good." Andrew nods approvingly. "Libby was hoping you'd be free. I think she feels outnumbered by us Donovans."

I smile politely, but quite frankly, Libby could invite forty friends and they'd still feel as if they were surrounded. The Donovans, en masse, are a raucous bunch. I discovered that at the wedding.

"Wouldn't miss it for the world," I lie.

Leaning across the table, I have an awkward goodbye hug with Libby before I head for the door. I make it all the way out onto the street before I realize I left my purse behind.

"Shit!"

Whirling around to go back inside, I run smack bang into a muscular body. I recognize the intoxicating woody scent of his cologne before I look up to see Rory Donovan staring down at me, his lips twisted in wry amusement.

"Forget something?" he asks. He holds his hand up and I see my black silk purse dangling from his finger.

"I was just coming to get that."

"Well, I've saved you the trouble, which was pretty decent of me since you've tried to ignore me all evening."

"I wasn't trying to ignore you. I was just busy checking there were no issues with the, eh, the lights or anything."

Rory raises an eyebrow at my lame response. "The lights looked fine to me."

From across the bar, his stare was intense, but up close it's even more powerful. It's as if he's stripping me bare with his gaze. I lower my eyes, unable to stand being examined so closely.

"I like to be thorough," I mutter. "May I have my purse, please?"

"Well, since you asked so nicely."

He holds out the purse and lets me take it. I'm surprised he's not going to tease me a little. Then I realize his brother, Aidan, is standing a few meters away waiting for him, so I guess he doesn't have time to play with me.

"Thank you," I tell him because I can't be rude to the man.

"My pleasure." The way he draws out the word *plea-*

sure makes my insides turn to jelly. "How do you plan to get home?"

"I'm going to hail a cab."

Rory tuts at me. "Unacceptable."

Before I can tell him I'm a big girl who's quite capable of getting herself home, he whips out his cellphone and starts pressing buttons.

"One of my guys will drive you home."

"That's not necessary."

"Yes," he says firmly, "it is, unless you'd rather I asked Aidan to make a detour to get you home safe."

I glance over his shoulder at his brother, who I find to be the most terrifying of the Donovans. While I'm wary of Rory, I am downright petrified of Aidan. Even if he didn't have a jagged scar running down his face as a testament to his life of violence, his chilling sternness would frighten me.

"No, it's fine."

"Aye," Rory says, "I thought not."

Luckily I don't have to stand next to his brooding masculinity for long as an older, gray-haired man with a potbelly appears on the sidewalk next to us. I have to stifle a laugh.

Red in the face, he obviously ran to get here. He's slightly sweaty and breathing heavily. Rory obviously picked the least attractive man he could think of to drive me home. He needn't worry. I'm not looking to sleep with any members of the Irish mob.

"This is Padraig," Rory tells me. "He'll get you home safely."

He turns and speaks quietly to the other man, who

nods in response to whatever instructions he was just given. Padraig goes to a dark blue Range Rover, parked a few yards down the street and gets into the driver's seat.

Rory takes my elbow in a firm, but not bruising grip and steers me to the car. He opens the back door and waits for me to climb onto the seat. Then he leans in close, his breath whispering over my ear.

"See you soon, Eleanor."

A shiver runs down my spine, born not of fear, but arousal. As he walks off, limping slightly due to some injury he suffered, I try to get a grip on myself.

My mind is telling me Rory Donovan is a bad idea, but my body says something entirely different. I guess I'm going to have to work extra hard to resist his charms because being with a man like that can only lead to trouble.

CHAPTER TWO

Rory

As I walk away from Eleanor, a twinge of pain shoots up my right leg. It's been more than two years now since some asshole shot me while trying to steal my wallet, but it still gives me trouble.

Apparently, that's my fault for not letting it heal properly after our family doctor removed the bullet and stitched me up. I don't know what anyone expected. I could hardly lie around in bed when every fiber of my being was calling out for revenge against the man who shot me.

Hearing him beg for mercy before I killed him was like the sweetest music to my ears. Still, I regret not resting my leg more in the weeks after I was hurt.

I groan as I ease myself into the passenger seat of Aidan's Mercedes. He glances my way, but knows better than to make a fuss. Big brother or not, I will smack him if he tries to baby me.

As Aidan pulls out into traffic, I look over my shoulder, hoping to catch one last glimpse of my red-haired beauty. I don't see her. Padraig's already moving off in the opposite direction.

"You need to fuck the lass and get her out of her system," Aidan says.

I shake my head. "Nah, I want to do this right. Can't risk upsetting Libby."

Eleanor being my new sister-in-law's friend is a convenient excuse for why I haven't made a move on her yet. I can pretend to everyone that I'm worried about creating tension with Andrew's wife if I hurt her friend.

It's not as if we need any more discord in the family. Aidan's wife, Madeline, is causing enough aggravation with her increasingly petulant behavior. She was always a bit of a brat, but a year ago, her behavior deteriorated after she killed a man. She and Libby were ambushed at a spa by our Bratva enemies, and Madeline shot one of them. It was a clear case of self-defense, but I guess that hasn't eased her conscience.

"So, what do you plan to do? Are you going to stare at the lassie until she cracks and spreads her legs for you?"

My jaw twitches in irritation at the way he talks about Eleanor.

"Maybe."

What my brother doesn't realize is that she isn't just some woman I want to fuck. I want to make her mine in every way, to possess her body and soul. It's the reason why I'm giving her time to get used to the idea of being with me. She knows I want her. Now I just have to wait until the right opportunity to claim her.

Aidan wouldn't understand that, though. Both he and my older brother, Ciaran, practically snatched their wives off the street. Andrew didn't have the most normal courtship with Libby, either. He married her as part of a deal our family made with her asshole of a father. I'd prefer to do things differently.

Of course, if Eleanor doesn't soften towards me soon, I'll have to take more drastic action. I may have a lot of patience, but I'm not a saint.

"So, anyway, what's going on?" I ask Aidan. "Did something happen?"

He told me there were matters we needed to discuss earlier this evening, but wanted to celebrate the opening of Andrew's new club before getting down to business.

"The Russians hit the warehouse in Camden."

"Fuck!" We move our guns through that warehouse. They come in from Eastern Europe and we store them for a couple of days before sending them on to our buyers in the United States. "Did they do much damage?"

"Some, but our latest shipment was delayed, so the warehouse was almost empty."

I turn in my seat to look at him.

"The shipment was delayed?" As his second-in-command, that's something I should have known about. "Why am I only just hearing this now?"

Aidan lifts a shoulder in a lazy shrug. "I forgot to tell you."

"You forgot?" Outrage and disbelief mingle in my tone. "How the hell could you forget to tell me?"

"I don't know. The call came in when you were out and Madeline distracted me, so I forgot."

"Madeline?" I scrub a hand over my face. "You have got to get to grips with that woman."

Aidan makes a scoffing sound. "Like you've got to grips with Eleanor?"

"That's different. She doesn't know enough to bring our whole family down, and I'm not allowing her to distract me from business."

Aidan nods wearily. "I know. You're right. I'll sort things out with Maddie."

I don't bother asking him how he intends to do that, but I wish him luck. His wife lives up to the stereotype of the fiery redhead. She's got a temper few men would want to be on the receiving end of.

In the beginning, the passion between her and Aidan was a positive thing. They sparked each other off and enjoyed sparring. Lately, it's begun to wear them both down.

My two older brothers and I have a bit of a thing for redheads. It's our mother's fault. Fancying herself a bit of a psychic, she once predicted that we'd find happiness with red-haired, green-eyed girls. I guess she wanted us to settle down with Irish lasses.

So far, it hasn't worked out too well. Aidan and Madeline are nobody's idea of the perfect marriage. On the other hand, my oldest brother, Ciaran, married Sorcha, whose hair is more of a reddish blonde, and they were very happy together. At least they were until he died in his sleep at far too young an age. Perhaps it will be third time lucky when I put a ring on Eleanor's finger.

Realizing I'm getting sidetracked, I get back to the original topic. "Were there any casualties at the warehouse?"

"Aye." Aidan sighs heavily. "Wee Niall took a bullet in the chest. He didn't make it."

"Fuck!" I liked Niall. He was only twenty. Thankfully, he wasn't married and had no kids that I'm aware of, but we'll need to provide for his mother now he's gone. "So, what are we doing about it?"

"Jacob and Manus are on it."

That catches me by surprise. My second youngest brother doesn't usually get involved in the rougher side of the family business. In fact, his work revolves around our legitimate enterprises. Manus is his bodyguard. He appointed himself to the role when Jacob was in high school. Fuck knows why. I suppose I should be grateful there's someone looking out for my brother, so I have one less person to worry about.

"Is that why he wasn't at the club tonight?" It's unlike Jacob to have missed the chance to support Andrew. The pair of them are close.

"Aye. They wanted to get straight on it. Manus is Niall's uncle, or cousin, or something. He's taking his death personally."

That explains why Jacob's getting involved. Loyalty runs both ways. Our people do whatever we require of them and in return, we make sure they're taken care of.

"Is Jacob up to it?" I love my younger brother, but neither Jacob nor Andrew has the same ruthless streak Aidan and I possess.

"He may not always act like it, but he's still our father's

son," Aidan says. "He'll bring one of those Bratva assholes in."

"Aye, you're right," I concede. Jacob's seen enough violence to know what's expected of him. Besides, Manus will do most of the dirty work. "So, what to we do in the meantime?"

"Well, I'm going home to get some sleep and you're going to see Trudy."

"Trudy?" She runs one of our most lucrative brothels. "What the fuck for?"

He'd better not be about to suggest I fuck one of the whores to get Eleanor off my mind, because that's not going to happen.

"A massage," Aidan says. "Don't think I haven't noticed your leg is hurting."

I could deny it, yell at him for trying to mollycoddle me, but I don't. The truth is, I am in considerable pain. There's an ache deep in the muscle of my right thigh and a massage will help ease that, if only in the short term.

"Aye, okay. A quick trip to Trudy's couldn't hurt."

Aidan gives me a sideways glance. "Maybe you could get your blue balls taken care of while you're there."

"Worry about your own blue balls, *deartháir*." I can't imagine Madeline is satisfying his baser needs right now. "I'm just fine."

"Are you?" Aidan says skeptically. "Because from where I'm sitting, you've found the woman you want and you're doing nothing to lock her down."

"I'll make a move when I'm good and ready."

"And when will that be?" he demands.

"Why is it such a big deal?" I can't understand why he's trying to push me.

"I just want to see everyone settled."

"Why? Are you dying?"

Aidan glares at me. "No, but I think it's time everyone stopped fucking around and started to build the kind of life our parents had. We need a solid foundation for the future."

The obvious retort would be to tell him to look to his own marriage first, but I know he's trying his best with Madeline, and I'm not about to hit him below the belt.

"Jacob's not even seeing anyone. Why don't you hassle him?"

"I've got plans for Jacob."

"Oh? And what are those?"

"You'll find out soon enough."

I hate it when my brother acts all mysterious, but if he doesn't want to share what he's up to, I'm not in the mood to try to pry it out of him.

He pulls up outside Trudy's house. As I'm getting out, he calls after me.

"If you want the girl, do something about it or I will, you hear me?"

"Aye, *deartháir*, I hear you."

Slamming the door, I walk away from the car. It pisses me off when Aidan acts like this. I have no idea why he's suddenly so keen for me to settle down, but if he thinks he's going to force my hand, he's mistaken. Eleanor will be mine when I decide the time is right and not before it.

CHAPTER THREE

Eleanor

STIFLING A YAWN, I tuck my hair behind my ears and try to focus on the laptop in front of me once more. The figures on the screen don't make sense. I measured everything so carefully, had Kenny, the lead contractor, look over the numbers for me, and somehow I've still ordered the wrong size of countertops for the kitchen area.

They arrived earlier this evening and they don't fit. They're three inches out, which is not a small mistake. I have no idea how I messed this up.

There has to be an explanation but, at two in the morning, I doubt I'm going to find it. I've been onsite for sixteen hours, and I'm too tired to see straight. This is the second night I've worked late on this project and the lack of sleep is starting to catch up with me.

Andrew Donovan wants to open the club in less than a fortnight, and I promised him everything was on track. This major setback could have serious repercussions. Everything I've done for him so far has run smoothly, so I don't know how he'll handle it if I can't deliver what I promised. I can't imagine he'll be pleased, though.

The pressure is intense, but there's nothing more I can do tonight. I shut down my laptop and get my blanket and pillow from the locker where I stashed them. Sometimes, when I work until the early hours, I make a bed on the sofa here in the office. I doubt Andrew would approve, but it's better than traveling across the city to get home and only having a couple of hours' sleep before I have to get ready to come back.

I drop my pillow onto the sofa and lay out my blanket. Then I head to the ladies' restroom. It was one of the first rooms we got up and running when we started the remodel on the club, thank goodness. After quickly taking care of business, I go to double check all the doors are locked. I secured the place after the last of the workmen left for the night, but I need to be certain I'm safe. Although we're in central London, the building feels quite isolated this late at night.

The front doors are locked, and the steel shutters are down. They haven't been opened all day, so I don't know why I felt compelled to check. I guess being alone makes me jittery. I live by myself, so you'd think I'd be used to it, but I'm not.

Once I've ensured everything at this side of the building is locked up tight, I head back through the main room of the club and walk down the corridor leading to the rear of the building. There's a door there leading out to the small parking lot the employees will use when the place opens.

As I walk along the corridor, switching off lights as I go, I hear a noise up ahead. Startled, I duck through the nearest door, into a storeroom.

Moments later, there's a scuffle outside. I hear a couple of different voices. A man is shouting, a pleading tone in his voice. He speaks a language I don't understand. It's Russian, I think.

Someone with a deep, throaty laugh mocks him. It takes a second or two before I catch a familiar voice, recognizing the Irish lilt of one of the Donovan brothers, though I don't know which one. They all have the accent, despite being largely brought up in London.

My heart pounds furiously as someone asks a question, addressing it to Aidan. So the boss of the family is here. He's never come to the site as far as I know. He has no reason to since this is Andrew's project.

I have a bad feeling about this. What are these men doing at what's more or less a construction site in the middle of the night? Whatever it is, it can't be good. I've seen enough Mafia movies to guess what's happening.

The men move on down the corridor and I relax a little. Though they passed by without detecting my presence, I still have to get out of here. If, as I suspect, they've brought someone here to hurt him, I don't want to be around to witness it.

All I have to do is get to the office, a few doors farther along the corridor, grab my purse and then slip out the fire exit. The nearest underground station is only five minutes away. I can hopefully be home and tucked up safely in bed within the hour. When I turn up for work tomorrow, I'll just act like nothing happened.

Taking care not to make a sound, I open the door to the storeroom and step out into the corridor. I close the door quietly behind me in case someone notices it's open, when it wasn't before.

I don't know much about the world of organized crime, other than what I've seen on TV, but I imagine these guys are observant. They'd need to be aware of their surroundings at all times so their enemies can't get to them.

As I creep along the darkened passageway, I wonder if I'm letting my imagination run away with me. There might be some perfectly legitimate reason for Aidan Donovan to be here, though I can't think what that would be.

Curiosity gets the better of me and I sneak back toward the main room of the club. I peer around the corner and have to stifle a gasp. Aidan Donovan is there along with his brother, Jacob and three others who I don't recognize. There's a man tied to a chair, his face bloodied.

"Give me a name," Aidan says.

The man spits a few words at him. I don't need to speak his language to recognize it's a curse. A sadistic grin twists Aidan's lips, like he was hoping that would be the response. Shit. This is about to get nasty. I have to get out of here.

As quietly as possible, I move back down the corridor. My stomach lurches as I hear the unmistakable whirr of a power drill coming to life. I hear a man's voice yelling 'nyet, nyet, nyet," and a second later, agonized screams fill the air.

Fear grips every part of me and my instinct to flee kicks in. Abandoning all thoughts of retrieving my purse, I run straight past the office and out through the back door. I wince as I shove it too hard, and it crashes against the wall. Fuck! I hope nobody heard that.

Crossing the street, I run for a couple of blocks, not really thinking about where I'm going. Then I spot a black cab coming in my direction. I frantically wave it down. Though I don't have my purse, I do have money at home to pay the fare. I can get into my house using the spare key I keep in a lockbox by the front door. Shit. What's the combination for that? I'm sure I'll remember by the time I get home.

"Are you alright, love?" the cab driver asks as I breathlessly give him my address.

"Yes, I'm fine."

He glances at me in the mirror, his furrowed brow suggesting he doesn't believe me. Thankfully, he doesn't push the subject. We drive in silence through the streets, and I try to figure out what my next move should be.

Perhaps it will be okay. I don't think anyone knows I was there tonight. If they did, they'd have chased after me, wouldn't they? There's no way they'd let a potential witness get away.

Then again, if they did hear something when I ran out, and went to investigate, they might have found my things in the office. If they put two and two together, they'll realize I was at the club. Fuck, this is a mess.

I can't risk them seeing me as a threat to them. I'll have

to lie low until I can speak to Libby. She'll help me smooth things over with the Donovans. At least, I hope she will, because there is no way I can hide from these people. I don't possess the necessary skills to evade them.

By the time we get to the street, where I pay an exorbitant rent for a 1980s terraced monstrosity, I've made up my mind what to do. I'll go and stay with my mother for a few days. I'll ask the cab driver to wait while I run into the house and pack a few things. Then I'll get him to take me to the railway station. There won't be a train to Canterbury, where my mother lives, until morning, but hopefully I'll be able to get a room at the hotel next to the station to wait it out.

As we pull up at the house, I scan the surrounding area in case there's anyone lurking in the bushes waiting to snatch me. I shake my head. I'm being ridiculous.

"Can you wait for me?" I ask the driver. "I need to grab a couple of things and then go back to the city."

"Yeah, alright, love," the gray-haired man replies. "Take as long as you need."

I'm sure he's saying that because the meter is running and not because he has infinite patience. I jump out of the cab and hurry to my front door. My hands shake as I try to enter the combination to open the lockbox.

It takes a couple of attempts before I'm able to retrieve the key. I also have some trouble slotting it into the lock, but eventually, I manage to get into the house.

Once inside, I close the door, lean back against it, and take a few deep breaths. I really need to calm down.

After a minute, I feel suitably composed. I go to my bedroom and grab my leather weekend bag from the top of the wardrobe. I stuff a few sets of clean underwear in it, along with a couple of pairs of jeans and some tops. Then I get my toothbrush and some other essentials from the bathroom. Although my mother always has plenty of toiletries on hand, I prefer my own shampoo to the cheaper brand she buys.

As soon as I'm packed, I take the money and my emergencies only credit card from the drawer in the nightstand. I hate to rack up debt, but if this doesn't qualify as an emergency, I don't know what would.

When I get back outside, I lock the door and turn to find the cab has gone. In its place, beneath the streetlight, is a black Range Rover. My heart lurches. Rory Donovan is leaning against its passenger door. Arms folded across his chest, he looks livid. He's dressed more casually than usual, in dark blue jeans and a black sweater. His hair is messy and, given the time of night, I think it's because he actually has just rolled out of bed. I didn't see him at the club, so someone must have called him.

He doesn't say a word, but opens the passenger door and tilts his head in a gesture for me to get into the car. I freeze, trying to decide what to do. There's no way I'd be able to unlock my front door and get back into the house. Rory would be on me before I can slot the key into the lock.

I could yell for help, but I don't know what good that would do. People around here mind their own business even if it sounds like someone is in trouble. Perhaps I could brazen it out and try to walk right past him.

Rory makes my mind up for me. He angles his body slightly and lifts up his sweater, revealing there's a gun tucked into his jeans. Shit. I might be able to outrun Rory, especially if his leg is hurting him tonight, but I'm definitely not faster than a bullet.

Holding my head high and trying not to look as terrified as I feel, I walk toward him. In an almost chivalrous gesture, he takes my bag from me and waits until I'm settled in my seat before shutting the car door. He puts my bag onto the back seat and gets into the driver's side.

"Seatbelt," he instructs as he turns the key in the ignition. He taps out a quick message on his cellphone, no doubt letting his brother know he's got me, and puts it in the pocket at the side of the door.

I fasten my seatbelt and clasp my hands together on my lap to stop them shaking as Rory pulls away from the curb.

"Are you not going to try to sell me some bullshit story about what you're doing sneaking about at this time of night?"

I shake my head. There is no explanation for Rory being at my home, other than that Aidan knows I was at the club. If I'm already caught, trying to deny that I was there is only going to make him angry.

"You going to tell me you didn't see anything?"

"No," I say quietly. "I saw plenty."

"Well, that's refreshing," Rory says. "I can't stand liars."

I'll need to bear that in mind. Perhaps if I'm honest and open with him, I can find a way out of this situation. As I try to think what to say to break the heavy silence between us, I realize he's heading for the motorway, leading out of the city.

"Where are you taking me?"

"Somewhere quiet."

I swallow hard. "Are you going to kill me?"

"Not tonight."

That's far from reassuring but, when he sees me shiver and leans over to put the heating on, I see a glimmer of hope. If he didn't care about me, at least in some small way, he wouldn't worry about my comfort, would he?

I lean my head against the window and watch as we slowly leave the city behind, driving out into the country-side. We eventually pull off the motorway and travel down a narrower road until we reach an enormous set of gates.

There's a guardhouse of sorts at the entrance and a large, muscular man with a buzz cut comes out to check who's in the car. The moment he sees Rory, he gives him a nod and signals for the gates to be opened.

We drive through, and a large building looms out of the darkness up ahead. I can't make out any details, but it appears to be a large house, like something out of a Jane Austen novel.

"What is this place?" I ask as we pull up at the bottom of a small flight of steps leading up to a big wooden door.

"Our country house," Rory says.

He switches off the engine and gets out of the car. I don't move, waiting for him to come around to my side and open the door. I remove my seatbelt and step out.

"Follow me." Rory's tone is terse, so I do as he asked without question. Until I get a better sense of things, I can't risk upsetting him.

We go inside, entering a huge hallway with a massive staircase sweeping down from the upper floor. It's dark, but I can see white marble gleaming in the moonlight coming in from a glass dome overhead.

Rory walks upstairs, fiddling with an app on his cellphone. Lights come on in the corridor as we reach it, so I guess that's what he was doing. We pass several doors, coming to a stop at the fifth on the right. Rory opens it. He grabs my arm and shoves me inside.

"I advise you to get some sleep while you can," he says.

Though the urge to ask him what he means by that is strong, I keep my mouth shut. He gives me a look I can't decipher, turns and leaves the room. In case there was any doubt I'm in trouble here, the scraping of a key in the lock tells me I'm a prisoner.

I turn to look around my surprisingly lavish cell. It's a lovely bedroom, with a pale blue carpet, cream walls and floral drapes. There's a gigantic bed with a padded headboard. The thick comforter spread out on it matches the curtains.

As I look around, I realize the room lacks any personal touches that would tell me who it belongs to. There's no artwork on the walls, no rugs, no cushions on the chintzy armchair by the window. It's probably not used very often. Everything looks like new.

There's a dressing table and a wardrobe, which I discover are empty when I go to open them. A door on the left side of the room leads into a small bathroom, the focal point of which is a soaker tub. It would probably do my aching muscles a world of good if I had a bath, but it seems really inappropriate to make myself at home.

With no other option, I decide to take Rory's advice and get some sleep. I cross over to the bed, kick off my shoes, and climb onto the bed. It's warm in this room, so I curl up on top of the comforter. I close my eyes, but I doubt I'll get any sleep. Thoughts are racing around my head and anxiety has my chest in a tight grip. It's going to be a long night.

CHAPTER FOUR

Rory

AFTER POURING myself a large glass of Jameson's, I sit on the sofa in the library and stare at the black leather bag on the table. It's the one Eleanor was carrying. I need to search it for weapons, cash or any other suspicious items, but I feel strangely conflicted about going through her things.

When Aidan roused me from my bed to tell me he thought she'd witnessed his interrogation of some Bratva fucker Jacob captured, I couldn't believe it. He explained how they'd found her purse in the office, along with a makeshift bed on the sofa that suggested she'd been planning to sleep in there.

That, in itself, is worthy of punishment. Spending the night alone in an empty building is reckless. I intend to take her to task for it.

Though Aidan said one of his men thought he heard someone running out the back door of the club, I still wasn't convinced it was Eleanor until I saw her leaving her house with that bag. The cab driver I paid off said she was planning to go back into the city. Where was she headed? She was clearly trying to run.

Foolish girl. We'd have hunted her to the ends of the Earth.

Setting down my glass, I lean forward and drag Eleanor's bag to the edge of the table. I unzip it and start to pull out her belongings. There's nothing much in it. I find a couple of changes of clothes, some lacy underwear, a toothbrush and some shampoo.

What I don't find is a passport or a large amount of cash, so I guess she wasn't planning to go far. Perhaps she was going to her mother's house. She lives in Kent, I believe.

When Eleanor started working for Andrew, we did a background check on her. Although she came recommended by Libby, my sister-in-law hadn't been around for very long and we weren't going to take her word for it that we could trust this woman. In our line of business, we have to be careful about the people we let into our sphere.

Not finding anything that suggests Eleanor has been working for the Bratva, the police or anyone else who might wish to do us harm, I conclude she was just in the wrong place at the wrong time. I zip up her bag, grab my glass and sit back, sipping the rich, smooth whisky.

I think about the woman upstairs in the spare bedroom. The information we got on Eleanor didn't reveal a lot.

Nobody knows who her father is. Her mother worked

as a cook at Libby's posh boarding school, and Eleanor was given a scholarship to attend.

Apparently, she was treated like crap the entire time she was there. Libby told me about it. People mocked her because her mother was the help.

They teased her about her secondhand clothes, her vivid red hair and freckles. I think that's probably left a mark on her. She's not the most confident woman I've ever met, though she works hard to disguise her lack of self-confidence behind a brisk, efficient manner. I can't wait to thaw her out a bit.

As I'm thinking about my red-headed beauty and all the things I'll do with her, footsteps echo in the hallway. I get up and walk to the desk, grabbing the gun I put in the drawer when I came in.

With tight security at the property, it's unlikely anyone would get in without my authorization, so I'm not overly concerned. That said, I expected to be alone here tonight, so it's best to be cautious.

The door opens and Jacob comes in, looking like shit. Usually immaculately turned out, he's scruffy, with a three-day growth of beard and dark shadows under his eyes.

His black shirt is several sizes too big, which leads me to believe Manus, the man-mountain who shadows him, lent him it. He's been tracking a mid-level member of the Bratva for the last few days and he doesn't seem to have had much sleep.

"What are you doing here?" I stash the gun back in the drawer.

The house belongs to the whole family, but it's not our

primary residence, and we usually only use it on the occasional weekend.

"Aidan sent me."

"What the fuck for? If he wants something, he's got a cellphone, hasn't he?"

Jacob shrugs. "He thought you might need someone out here with you."

To handle one woman? Aidan obviously doesn't trust me with Eleanor.

I set aside my annoyance as I watch my younger brother slump onto the sofa I just got up from. He looks green around the gills and I realize Aidan had more than one purpose in sending him out here. It's not just that he wants Jacob to make sure I can deal with Eleanor, it's that he wants me to make sure our brother is okay with what happened tonight.

Jacob is more sensitive than the rest of us, and he isn't used to dealing with the rougher aspects of our business. I guess capturing the Bratva asshole has been harder on him than Aidan thought it would be.

"Want one of these?" I ask, holding up my glass.

"Aye, make it a large one."

I go to pour him a drink from the bottle on the table by the window, topping up my glass at the same time.

"Here." I hand him his whisky and drop onto the sofa opposite him. "So, what happened with the Russian?"

"He gave up his entire crew and we know which of the bastards shot Niall.

"Good." We can single out Niall's killer for special treatment.

Jacob takes a sip of his drink and then shakes his head. His face is pale, drawn. He looks tortured.

"It was a bloody mess. I've never seen anything like it."

I grimace, imagining how it must have been. Aidan has a range of techniques he can employ to get information out of a man and none of them are for the faint-hearted.

"How do you do it?" Jacob asks.

That's a million dollar question. My first taste of violence came when I was thirteen years old and I stumbled in on my father showing my older brothers exactly how our family deals with traitors.

I wish I could say I was horrified, but I wasn't. Watching that man bleed, I felt nothing but pride for the way my father took care of us. He was brutal in eliminating threats, hurting only those who deserved it. I've tried to be just like him, doing whatever is necessary to protect the people I love.

"You learn to deal with it, I guess."

"I couldn't stay to the end." Jacob twists his glass around in his hand. "I walked out."

He blows out a breath and his shoulders slump in defeat.

"You're worried about what the others will think of you?"

"The guys, no. Manus already told me it doesn't matter, that nobody expects me to join in, but I don't want to let Aidan down. I don't want to be the weak link in the family."

"You're not the weak link, kid. If you had to step up, you would."

Jacob raises a questioning eyebrow, so I carry on.

"And you don't have to worry about Aidan. He loves you and he's proud of you. He doesn't care if you don't want to get your hands dirty."

"Aye, maybe, but I still feel like a pussy. You and Andrew would have seen it through."

"Andrew would have hated it as much as you did." My youngest brother also has an aversion to violence, though he does step up when he has to. "And don't ever compare yourself to me. I'm not someone you want to emulate."

The air between us thickens with tension. I don't do heart to heart conversations with my brothers for this very reason. It gets awkward quickly when we stray into emotional territory. I stare into my glass as if the amber liquid it contains is going to reveal the secrets of the universe to me.

"So what are you going to do with Eleanor?" Jacob asks, eventually.

"Haven't decided."

He eyes me speculatively. "You like her, don't you?"

The question catches me off guard. If he'd asked me if I want to fuck her, that would have been easy to answer. There hasn't been a day since I first laid eyes on her at Andrew's wedding that I haven't thought about her on her knees before me with those plump red lips wrapped around my cock. But do I like her? That's trickier.

"Yeah, maybe."

"What will you do if Aidan orders you to kill her?" Jacob asks. "Will you do it?"

"No, I won't. We owe each other loyalty, Jacob, not blind obedience," I reply. "Besides, he doesn't want me to kill her. He wants me to marry her."

Jacob's eyes widen. "You too, huh? You know he's trying to get me to babysit some heiress. He thinks we'll hit it off."

It seems our brother is serious about his matchmaking efforts. I have no idea what's got into him lately, but if he's convinced us settling down will help the family, he's not going to rest until it happens.

Then something occurs to me, that should have before now. It's strange that they chose Andrew's new club as the venue for interrogating the Bratva asshole they captured. I'll bet my shirt Aidan knew Eleanor would be there. He set her up, set us both up. If I don't want to claim her, the only option is to put a bullet between her eyes and he knows I won't let that happen. Fuck!

Tamping down my fury at being maneuvered into this fucked-up situation, I focus on Jacob.

"What heiress?"

"Helena Spencer of Spencer Construction."

I know the name, but can't place it. "What's Aidan's connection to her?"

"He's her legal guardian, apparently."

I bark out a laugh. "Legal guardian. How old is this fucking girl?"

"Almost twenty-five."

"And she has a guardian? What is this, the fucking Middle Ages?"

Jacob shrugs. "Her parents died when she was seventeen. Their will named Ciaran as her guardian. Apparently, they trusted him with their daughter. When he died, the responsibility passed to Aidan."

This makes no sense.

"If he's had responsibility for this girl all this time, how come none of us have ever laid eyes on her?"

"Well, I'm guessing he's been pretty hands-off in his role as guardian."

I shake my head in disbelief.

"Un-fucking-believable."

"I know." Jacob sets down his glass and gets to his feet. "I'm going to get some shut-eye."

As Jacob heads off to bed, I finish my drink and open up my phone, sending Aidan a message to tell him he's a fucking wanker. Let him figure out why. There's any number of reasons.

I push to my feet and subdue a yawn. My fucking leg hurts again and I limp upstairs toward my bedroom. As I pass Eleanor's room, I pause for a moment and listen. There's not a sound coming from within. I wonder if she'll manage to sleep tonight. I hope for her sake she can. Tomorrow won't be easy for her. If she wants to survive, she's going to have to be tough.

CHAPTER FIVE

Eleanor

As SUNLIGHT FLOODS into the room, I slowly peel my eyes open. My vision is blurry and it takes several long seconds before I can focus enough to see my surroundings. A part of me had hoped I would wake this morning in my own bed, to discover I'd had a bad dream, but it seems I really am here, a prisoner in the Donovan's country mansion.

I wonder, briefly, what happened to the man they tortured last night and then set thoughts of him aside. There are more pressing things for me to worry about, like my own fate.

I get up from the bed and go to the window. I try to open it, but it's nailed shut. It doesn't matter. There's a long drop to the ground and I'm not the type to go shimmying down drainpipes. That would require a better head for heights than the one that's on my shoulders.

Though I hate the thought of being trapped in this room, I can't help but admire the view. There's a walled garden down below, laid out in a very traditional style with lawns and flower beds. There's a little pergola with a wrought-iron table and a couple of chairs in it. That would be a great spot to enjoy afternoon tea.

Beyond the formal garden there's a wild meadow, carpeted with daisies and buttercups. It's surrounded by woodland and who knows what comes after that,

It would be easy to slip into a daydream while gazing out into the beauty of nature, but the scraping of a key in the lock on my door startles me. I turn, heart racing, as the door swings open.

Expecting Rory, I'm surprised when his younger brother, Jacob, comes into the room, carrying a tray. In black sweatpants and a white t-shirt, and with his face unshaven, he looks uncharacteristically disheveled.

"Brought you some breakfast," he says, as if the plate of bacon and eggs, the toast, orange juice and coffee required explanation.

"Why? Where's Rory?"

"He's on the phone with Aidan."

"They're discussing me?" I ask, and Jacob nods. "Am I...will I make it out of this?"

Jacob sets the tray down on the dressing table, the only available space to put it other than on the bed.

"I've gotta be honest with you, I don't know." He rubs the back of his neck, apparently ill at ease with the situation. He steps back toward the door. "Eat your breakfast before it goes cold."

As he turns to leave, I call out to him. "Jacob."

He spins around to face me.

"What do I do?" I ask wishing my voice hadn't taken on that note of desperation. "How do I get through this?"

"By doing whatever Rory tells you to do."

The sense of being trapped intensifies at the thought of being at Rory's command. My eyes water as I blink back tears. I don't know how Rory feels about me right now. I have no idea what he'll expect of me.

Jacob tilts his head, gesturing toward the food he brought me. "Seriously, eat your breakfast before it gets cold. The eggs are amazing."

As he walks out and locks the door behind him, despair claws at me. I go to the bathroom and hover over the toilet, anticipating that my sudden nausea will lead to me throwing up, but it doesn't. I wash my hands and head back out into the bedroom, taking a seat at the dressing table. If I'm not going to get sick, I might as well eat my breakfast.

Perhaps I should assume it's a good sign they decided to feed me this morning. Unless, of course, this is someone's idea of a suitable last meal. I dismiss the thought. Rory brought me out here for a reason. If he'd wanted to kill me, he would have taken me to some abandoned warehouse, not to his family's country home. At least, I hope that's the case.

Trying not to look at myself in the mirror, because I'm a complete mess, I scoop up a forkful of scrambled eggs. Jacob was right. They are delicious, rich, buttery and seasoned perfectly. I wonder whether he or Rory cooked this and then decide they probably have a housekeeper.

The coffee is a bit strong for my tastes, but I drink it

anyway. The orange juice is sweet and has some pulp in it, so I guess it's freshly squeezed. It's really refreshing, and I feel invigorated after drinking it. That's good. I suspect I'll need my wits about me when Rory finally shows face.

Almost as if I've conjured him up, the door opens and the man himself walks in. I set down my knife and fork and swivel around on the stool to face him. He looks amazing this morning in black dress pants that hug his muscular thighs and a white shirt with the sleeves rolled up to his elbows. His forearms are strong and tanned and he's wearing a wristwatch, something I find incredibly sexy. A lot of men rely on their phones to tell them the time these days, but you can't beat a nice watch with a thick leather strap.

I startle as Rory drops something on the floor at my feet. It's my weekend bag.

"Tidy yourself up," he instructs. "My sister-in-law will be here in an hour."

"Libby?" I ask hopefully.

Rory shakes his head. "Sorcha."

I don't really know Sorcha. We've met a couple of times and she's been polite, friendly, but sort of detached. She seems like the perfect mob widow to me, keeping close to her late husband's family and never putting a foot wrong. It's unlikely I'd be able to persuade her to help me escape.

"She'll have a couple of dresses for you to try on. Pick one and don't give her any shit."

"Okay." I glance up at his sternly handsome face. His jaw is clenched tight, like he's barely holding onto his temper. "Why is she bringing dresses?"

"Because we're getting married this morning," he grits out.

My brow furrows. "You and Sorcha?"

The look Rory gives me suggests he thinks it was a stupid question, which I guess it was. He clarifies nonetheless.

"You and me."

My stomach lurches.

"You can't be serious."

"Deadly." Rory puts his hand in his pocket and pulls out a red velvet ring box. "You're a witness, a threat to my family. We don't like loose ends, so there are two ways your day can end, in wedded bliss or eternal rest."

The grim way he says *wedded bliss* makes me think the second option is actually the more appealing one. He thrusts the ring box at me and I take it. I open the box to find a delicate platinum band with an oval cut emerald surrounded by glistening diamonds. It's stunning but I frown deeply as I consider what accepting it would mean.

"Don't you like it?"

I can't be certain, but I think I detect a note of anxiety in Rory's voice. It matters to him if I like the ring.

"It's beautiful. I love it."

"Good, because it's that, or a bullet. Take your pick."

"The ring," I say when I realize he's staring expectantly at me, waiting for an answer. "I pick the ring."

"Then put it on."

Tears burn behind my eyes as I take the ring out of the box and slip it onto my finger. I never really fantasized about a man proposing to me one day, but however I thought someone would ask me to marry them, it wasn't like this. The ring is a little tight, but I manage to push it over my knuckle.

"There." I hold my hand up for Rory to see.

He stares at the gorgeous piece of jewelry now adorning my left hand for a moment. A myriad of emotion flits across his face — pride, lust, rage — before his features settle into an inscrutable expression once more.

"Good. Now, behave when Sorcha gets here. You're already looking at a punishment. You don't want to increase it."

Before I can ask him what the hell he means by punishment, he marches from the room, slamming the door behind him. A moment later, the key turns, locking me in once more. I pick up a piece of bacon from my plate. It's cold but still deliciously salty and savory. I eat it and gulp down the last dregs of coffee. A throbbing behind my eyes tells me I'm in for a headache.

Hoping that a nice warm bath will ease the tension, I go to the bathroom and put the stopper in the tub. I start the water running and then strip off my clothes. I look around for bubble bath or something else to make the water smell nice, but there's just a bar of soap available.

Perhaps when I've been upgraded from captive to wife, I can ask for some scented oils. I scoff at the naïve thought that being Rory's wife is going to be any different to being his prisoner. He's not marrying me out of love, or even desire. It's to keep me close so he can control me, keep me from talking.

On that depressing note, I sink into the water, close my eyes and hope that by some miracle my troubles will be washed away.

CHAPTER SIX

Eleanor

RORY TOLD me to expect Sorcha in an hour, but it feels like it's been twice that long. I'm lying on the bed, staring at the ceiling, when I finally hear them outside my door. They're speaking in hushed tones, but I can tell they're bickering. I sit up on the bed, the ends of my frizzy hair damp and bedraggled after my bath. Though I can't make out the conversation, I do hear something about Sorcha getting here as soon as she could. They're arguing about her being late, it seems.

I feel kind of bad for Sorcha but, when the door opens, and she glides into the room, there's no hint of tension on her face. She flashes me a radiant smile, and I can't help hating her a little.

The woman is a goddess. At least five foot ten in her bare feet, she's long-limbed and slender. Her skin practically glows and she reminds me of a young Grace Kelly with her perfectly symmetrical features.

I've never seen her look unpolished and now is no exception. She's wearing a vibrant yellow dress that shouldn't work so well with her strawberry blonde hair and black ankle boots that push her closer to Rory's height.

He walks in behind her, carrying several bags. There are a couple of boxes under his arm. He dumps everything on the end of the bed, picks my breakfast tray up from the dressing table and leaves, without so much as glancing in my direction. I get the sense he's mad at me, but I can't see how that's justified. I'm the victim of circumstance here.

"I wouldn't try it." Sorcha must see the way I'm eyeing the door. "If you run, he'll bring you back and it won't be pretty."

"You speak from experience, do you?" My tone is more hostile than I intended.

"Yes," Sorcha replies. "I do."

If I knew her better, I'd ask her for more information, but I'm reluctant to pry into her personal life.

"Shouldn't I at least try to get away?"

Sorcha shakes her head. "Take it from me, you're better off just smiling prettily until you can find a way to turn this to your advantage."

She's right. I need to play along with Rory until I get a better grasp of my situation. If I can get him to trust me, it will be easier to slip away. I get up from the bed.

"So, what pretty things have you brought for me?"

"Well," she says with an apologetic grimace. "I didn't really know your style. I've only ever seen you in workwear."

Considering I've seen Sorcha at a wedding and two nightclub openings, that stings. I guess she's right, though. Even my special occasion wardrobe is fairly utilitarian. Since I spend eighty percent of my income on rent and utility bills and the rest on pesky life-sustaining necessities like food, there isn't a lot of money left for clothes.

"I'm sure whatever you picked will be lovely."

Sorcha goes to the pile of stuff Rory left on the bed and retrieves a black garment bag from the bottom. She places it on top of the pile and unzips it, carefully removing a gorgeous swathe of white silk and lace.

"It's a proper wedding dress," I marvel as she holds the hanger up so I can see its full length.

"Of course. I know this isn't a conventional wedding, but I wasn't going to let you get married in a burlap sack."

I approach the dress, almost as if I'm afraid it's going to bite me, and run my hand over the gloriously silky fabric. It's a beautiful gown with a corset style bodice and a long silk skirt overlaid with the most delicate lace.

"Try it on."

Sorcha doesn't have to ask twice. I take the dress from her and head into the bathroom. After carefully hanging it on the door, I strip off my jeans, shirt and bra, because I won't need it with this dress.

Thankfully, the underwear I packed is lacy because it would feel weird trying on such a gorgeous dress with granny pants. I step into the dress, taking care not to stand on the hem, and pull it up my body.

It feels so luxurious, the fabric caressing my skin. The back is fastened with a row of delicate silk-covered buttons that I can't possibly manage by myself. Clutching the bodice to me, I step out into the bedroom. Sorcha grins broadly and I know she's thinking the same thing I am, that this is the dress.

"Can you help with the buttons?" I ask.

"Yes, of course."

I give her my back and pull my long, unruly hair out of the way so she can fasten the buttons. It takes several minutes, and she curses a couple of times as she struggles to get the tiny buttons through the hooks. Eventually, she succeeds. The dress fits snugly. I let my hair down and turn to face her.

"It's gorgeous." Sorcha steps back to get a better look. "It could have been made for you."

"It does feel perfect, but it's a little long."

"The shoes will fix that. Now, let's get the dress off you so I can do your hair and make-up."

"Can't we do that with the dress on?"

"No. I'm not risking it getting dirty. Besides, I bought you some really nice panties and stockings and you won't get those on without crushing the dress."

"Okay." I turn my back to Sorcha once more and she begins the laborious task of unbuttoning me.

"This is so fiddly," she grumbles, "and I have thin fingers. Andrew will never get you out of this without tearing it."

"You think he's going to be undressing me?"

"Of course, unless you plan to consummate the marriage fully clothed."

Sorcha's words knock me sideways. Until this moment, I hadn't thought about what this whole thing means. I latched onto marrying Rory as the acceptable option far too easily. I didn't protest, didn't put up any sort of fight. Before I even had time to formulate a question in my head, I was slipping the ring on my finger, making my choice. Am I fucking insane? I must be.

Suddenly, I can't catch my breath. Panic grips me and I feel as if I'm going to be sick. I somehow manage to get out of my dress, leaving it on the floor as I sprint to the bathroom. I make it to the toilet just in time to be violently ill. Heaving sobs wrack my body as I consider the ultimatum Rory gave me. Marriage or death. Are those really my only options? That can't be right.

I barely saw anything at the club last night. As a witness, I'd be useless since I can't describe the man who was tied to the chair and I don't actually know what happened to him. My life cannot be forfeit when I don't really have information that could bring the Donovans down.

"There must be another way," I say as Sorcha comes into the room.

She crouches next to me, a look of concern on her face.

"Don't do this to yourself, Eleanor." She puts an arm around my shoulders and pulls me in for a hug. "I know you're feeling trapped right now, but if you marry Rory, he'll be good to you. I know he will."

"But I don't want this," I protest. "I don't want Rory fucking Donovan."

"Well, tough shit."

Startled, I pull back from Sorcha and meet Rory's dark glare as he looms large in the doorway. He has a jacket and tie on now. It's incredibly sexy, but I can't ignore how livid he is.

"Get off the fucking floor, get dressed and be at the fucking church on time. If you're not there, I'll drive to Canterbury and slit your mother's throat. Do you understand me?"

"You're a monster!" I spit at him.

"Yes, sweetheart, I am. Now, I'll ask you one more time. Do you understand me?"

"Yes, I understand."

Rory nods briskly, turns and storms off. Both Sorcha and I jump as the bedroom door slams shut.

"He doesn't mean it," Sorcha says as she sees the look of pure shock on my face. "He wouldn't really do that."

"Yes," I tell her as I struggle to my feet, "I think he would."

I quickly wash my face and dry off with a towel before returning to the bedroom. Like it or not, I have a wedding to get to.

CHAPTER SEVEN

Rory

Despite the warning I gave Eleanor, she's late. According to my watch, she should have been here ten minutes ago. I know she hasn't tried to run, because Sorcha would have let me know. That means she's stalling, deliberately pushing it to see how I'll respond. She's not going to like the result of playing games with me.

"Are you nervous, son?" Father McKinlay asks.

He's been our family priest since he baptized my brothers and me when we were babies. He conducted Ciaran's wedding and his funeral. Father McKinlay also officiated at Aidan and Andrew's marriage ceremonies, which came about under far from conventional circumstances with less than willing brides.

Yet here he is once more, apparently oblivious to the fact my marriage is not the result of a love match.

"No, just impatient."

He gives me a knowing nod, imagining no doubt my impatience is because I can't wait to be alone with my new bride. In fact, what's irritating me is that my leg is getting stiff as I stand here. I shift my weight from right to left and back again, wincing as a pain shoots through me. Clenching my fists, I breathe in and out through my nose in slow, measures breaths until the ache subsides.

"She's here," Jacob announces as he walks up the short aisle to join me. He frowns as he looks me up and down, taking in the tension in my body. "Are you okay, *deartháir*?"

"I'm fine," I reply, my tone unconvincing.

Though I'm trying hard not to view this union that's been forced upon me in a romantic light, I can't resist turning to watch Eleanor as she walks down the aisle with Sorcha. No, she doesn't walk, she floats. There's a quiet, serene beauty about her that's almost ethereal, like one of the faerie folk my mother used to tell us about when we were kids.

Eleanor is simply stunning with her hair pulled back off her face. Her white dress hugs her curves, managing to make her both alluring and innocent at the same time. It makes me want to dirty her up a bit.

As she draws closer, I feel a pang of guilt. With only the barest amount of make-up on, she looks incredibly young and I remember she is fifteen years my junior. I quickly shove my regrets aside when she glares defiantly at me. Little minx. She'll pay for that later.

Grabbing her hand, I pull her hard against me.

"Behave yourself," I warn her.

I allow her to step back, putting some space between us, but I hold on tight to her hand. Father McKinlay begins the ceremony and Eleanor resolutely keeps her focus on a spot on the wall straight ahead of her. I recite my vows without hesitation, but when Eleanor's turn comes, she falters.

Her voice quiet, she stumbles over the words. I tighten my grip on her hand, both to lend her some strength and to warn her not to do anything stupid. I couldn't bring myself to kill her, but Aidan won't hesitate to track her down if he thinks she's a threat to the family.

When I slide the simple wedding band onto her finger, she finally looks up to meet my gaze. She nervously bites her bottom lip as Father McKinlay pronounces us man and wife. I curve my hand around the back of her head and pull her close. There's nothing tender about the way I kiss her. It's rough and brutal. Eleanor whimpers and I pull back, not because I'm afraid of hurting her, but because I like it too much and we have an audience.

As I march her over to the table to sign the documents making our marriage official, Jacob and Sorcha follow in our wake. I scrawl my name on the certificate and hand Eleanor the pen.

"You've come this far," I whisper to her. "Don't make a stupid mistake now."

Her hand shakes as she signs. Jacob and Sorcha add their names as witnesses to this sordid affair and I thank Father McKinlay for his work here today. As we make the short walk back along the aisle, I try to remember a more miserable occasion, but I can't think of one.

Even at Aidan's wedding, where Madeline had to be

marched to the altar by armed men, we had family and friends in attendance. There was a celebration afterwards.

I glance down at Eleanor and realize she hasn't even got a fucking bouquet. Though neither of us wants to be here, I should have done better for her.

We step outside to where two cars are waiting. One will take my new bride and me back to the mansion, where we'll spend the next few days getting to know each other better. The other, driven by Manus, will take my brother and Sorcha home to London.

I allow my sister-in-law to drag Eleanor off to the side. She throws her arms around my new wife's neck and whispers something to her, words of comfort, no doubt.

"Don't forget dinner on Thursday night," Jacob tells me. "Everyone will want to congratulate you and your new bride."

Everyone will want to see if I have her under control, more like. I grimace at the thought of bringing Eleanor to her first family dinner so soon, but it's Andrew's birthday and I can't miss it.

"We'll be there."

I reclaim my bride from Sorcha and lead her toward the Audi SUV that's waiting for us. Opening the back door, I help her inside, the very model of chivalry. Aidan may have pushed me into this union before I was ready for it, but I intend to do right by my bride, provided she learns to obey me.

"We'll see you soon," Sorcha calls after me. I hear the concern in her voice. It's a little insulting. She knows that whatever else I am, I'm not a man who hurts women. Or perhaps it's me she's worried about. Maybe she thinks Eleanor will stab me in my sleep. I'd liked to see her try.

I climb into the back of the car with my wife and James drives us back to the house. There's complete silence and I'm grateful the journey only takes six minutes.

When we pull to a stop, I jump out first and help Eleanor to climb down from the back seat. Her movements are hampered by her dress.

Putting my arm around her waist, I lead her into the house. She seems to think we're heading upstairs as she pulls in that direction, but I take her along the corridor to my study. I position her in front of the desk while I go to sit behind it. As I stare at her, she shuffles awkwardly from one foot to the other.

"What?" The word comes out as a squeak, so she clears her throat and tries again. "What are we doing?"

"We need to get a few things straight." I take a ruler from the drawer and smack it down on the desktop, causing Eleanor's eyes to widen. "Neither of us chose this marriage, but it doesn't mean I don't want it to work."

"Okay," she says warily.

"So you'll need to understand a few things about the man you married."

She clasps her hands in front of her, a prim gesture that matches the snooty tone she adopts.

"Let me guess. You like to be in control. Your word is law, and I'd better obey. You don't do love, so I shouldn't expect it."

I raise my eyebrows at that. "I'm more than capable of loving people, Eleanor."

"Really? A man like you."

I don't bother to ask what she means by "a man like me" because I can imagine what she thinks.

"I may occasionally have to commit acts that would turn most men's stomachs, Eleanor, but I was raised in a loving family. I care deeply for those who are loyal to me and rip those who hurt them to pieces. Do you understand?"

She nods, but the crease at the bridge of her nose suggests she's perplexed.

"Did you marry me because you're in love with me?"

I bark out a laugh. "No, my dear wife, I married you because I wanted to fuck you more than I wanted to shoot you."

If it's possible, her eyes grow even wider.

"You married me for sex?"

"And because I like you." It's a decent foundation for a marriage, something to build on. "But that could change at any moment."

"What do you mean?"

"I mean that if you give me trouble, if you displease me, I might change my mind."

Eleanor blinks rapidly as she digests what I've just said. She chews on her bottom lip, uncertainty leaking from every pore in her body. Then she nods as if she's made her mind up about something.

She steps around to my side of the desk. Tugging down her corset, she reveals her pale, creamy breasts, tipped with rosy nipples. She drops to her knees beside me and I swivel my chair around to face her. As she reaches out to unbuckle my belt, a tremor runs through her.

Anger surges through me. I want her, but not like

this. There's no pleasure to be gained in making her submit when she's carrying such an air of defeat. It's pathetic.

"Get up," I snarl.

She pushes to her feet, tripping over the hem of her dress. She steadies herself and looks down at me, eyes glistening with unshed tears.

"What did I do wrong?" she asks. "I was only trying to please you."

Something insides me snaps. I surge to my feet, grab the ruler and push Eleanor face down over the desk. I whip her skirt up and rip off her flimsy lace panties.

My cock stiffens when I see the pretty ribbons tied at the top of her stockings. I smack her ass, three times, leaving a satisfying pink hue on her skin. She shrieks each time the ruler cracks against her butt.

"Stop, please, you're hurting me."

"That's the fucking point. It's a punishment."

Holding her down, I spank her two more times and she struggles to get up.

"Quit moving!"

I bring the ruler down on her ass once more, then toss it aside. Kicking her legs apart, I position myself behind her. I run a finger along her slit, finding her wet and ready for me.

"No, please," she wails as I unbuckle my belt. "Not like this."

I let go of her, and she stumbles away from the desk. She turns to face me, the tracks of tears staining her pale cheeks. My hand shoots out to wrap around my tauntingly innocent bride's throat. She gasps as I back her against the wall. As I tighten my grip, her hands fly up to try to pull me off her.

"Please, Rory," she cries. "Don't hurt me."

"I can do what I want to you whenever I want." The menace in my voice makes her quiver in fear. It's intoxicating.

"I know." She claws at my hand as she tries to pry my fingers off her throat. I squeeze a little harder, just enough to warn her to stop. Her hands drop to her sides. "Please, Rory, I'm begging you. Don't hurt me."

Disgusted with her, with myself, I loosen my grip and shove her away.

"You reek of desperation," I spit at her. "Go to your room and don't come out until you grow a backbone."

She doesn't need to be told twice. Whirling around, she picks up her skirts and stumbles from the room. I stare at the door for a moment, my breathing ragged. Then I go and pour myself a whisky, a large one. I down it in a single gulp. That was not the way I intended to start my marriage. I drop onto the chair behind my desk and scrub a hand across my face. What the fuck have I just done?

CHAPTER EIGHT

Eleanor

When I finally stop crying, I fall asleep. I must be exhausted, because when I open my eyes again, the first thing that strikes me is that the room is dark. The curtains are drawn. They weren't before.

Did someone come to check on me? I like to think Rory might have enough of a conscience to worry that he hurt me, but who knows?

Without a watch or my cellphone, I have no idea what time it is. I get up from the bed and go to open the curtains. There's still some light in the sky, so I'm guessing it's not too late.

Leaning against the window frame, I look out over the magnificent gardens and try to make sense of all that's happened today. Sorcha advised me to try to make Rory happy, and I really thought that was what I was doing when I got down on my knees for him. He reacted with such rage and disappointment that it startled me. I guess the way to win him over is not with easy submission.

I replay all that he said to me today. It's clear his hand was forced when he married me, but he wanted to do it all the same. The problem, I think, is that he's a man who likes control. He wanted to set his own agenda and my being at the club the other night ruined whatever plans he had to seduce me.

As I recall the venom when he said I reeked of desperation, I actually flinch. I don't know what he expected. In this situation, how could I be anything but desperate? He told me not to show face until I've grown a backbone. I realize what he wants. He doesn't like timid women. He was interested in me before, when I refused him.

Standing up for myself is the way to gain his respect and, eventually, his trust. He prefers strong women, yet he also wants me to obey and punish me when I step out of line. It's sort of bewildering.

That brings me to my second point of confusion. I enjoyed being spanked. I even kind of like that my ass is still sore, that it chafes when the fabric of my dress rubs against it. Rory's punishment hurt and I was humiliated, but I was also aroused. That's so twisted, I'm not sure I can even begin to untangle it.

Unraveling the mysteries of my desires is going to have to wait. My stomach rumbles and I need to eat. I reach around to try to unbutton my dress, but it's impossible, so I just straighten out the corset and leave it on. Not bothering to put my shoes back on, I go to the door. Shit. What if it's locked? I guess I'll have to try shouting until Rory comes to me.

I turn the handle and the door opens. Almost tiptoeing, I head downstairs into the gorgeous hallway. Taking the corridor to the left, I walk slowly along, peering through open doors. This house is vast, and it's immaculately decorated. I wonder which of the Donovan women was responsible for this. Maybe they all had a hand in it. I definitely see touches of Libby's girly style in the squishy sofas and pink cushions in one of the sitting rooms.

There's art on the walls that probably costs more than I'll earn in a lifetime. I guess crime does pay. Maybe I'm being unfair. The Donovans own several successful, legitimate businesses as well. The thought occurs to me that I need to stop thinking of them as a separate entity. I'm one of them now, whether I like it or not.

When I eventually reach the kitchen, I'm not surprised to discover it's enormous. It has a huge island in the center with a marble top. There's a stove with eight burners. The clock on the oven tells me it's seven thirty. Hmm, I thought it was a bit later than that.

I look in the huge, American-style refrigerator and find it packed with veggies and other good things. The pantry is also fully stocked. I could make almost anything I wanted, but right now I'm craving something spicy.

When I come across a tub of Thai curry paste, I decide that's what I'll make. I find a bowl and soak some jasmine rice while I start to chop up the vegetables. Assuming Rory will like this, since there are several Asian ingredients in the pantry, I make enough for two.

I've got the rice cooking and the veggies frying when Rory comes into the room. He sits at one of the high stools at the island and watches me as I move from the stove to the refrigerator, my skirt swishing around my ankles.

"Why are you still wearing that?" he asks me.

I grab the open tin of coconut milk I found and sniff to make sure it's still okay before heading back to the stove.

"The buttons are fiddly and I couldn't reach them. I didn't want to risk damaging the dress."

Rory scrunches his nose up. "But you're cooking in it."

I look down and see some green splatters on the skirt. Shit. Why didn't I think to find an apron, or wrap a towel around my waist?

"Guess I didn't think that through," I say lightly.

"Whatever it is you're making, it smells good."

"Thai green curry. I haven't put any meat in it. I hope that's okay."

His eyebrows shoot up. "You made some for me?"

"Yeah, I thought you might be hungry, too."

Rory nods. "I could eat a scabby horse."

I laugh. "My granny used to say that."

"Was she a red-headed beauty like yourself?"

Flirtatious Rory has come to dinner, it seems. His eyes sparkle with mischief, and I wonder if we're going to be able to put what happened earlier behind us.

"Yeah, she was Scottish and very proud of her ginger hair."

"I wouldn't call yours ginger."

Rory stares at me and my cheeks heat under his scrutiny. That is a definite curse of my flame red hair and porcelain skin. I can't hide my blushes.

There's a moment of tension between us. It's not like it

was in his study earlier. This time, the silence is laden with nervous anticipation. Rory clears his throat.

"Do you need me to do anything?"

"Maybe set the table and open a bottle of wine."

I saw an impressive wine fridge in the pantry, but I didn't want to be presumptuous and help myself. Rory immediately goes and fetches a bottle.

"Pinot Grigio alright with you?" he asks, as he sets it down on the island while he retrieves a corkscrew from a drawer next to the sink.

"Yes, lovely."

He opens the wine, finds a couple of glasses, and takes them to the wooden table at the far side of the room. After opening the wine, he gets out some silverware and napkins and sets the table. He takes plates from a cabinet next to the dishwasher and places them on the table.

The curry looks good, and the rice is nice and fluffy, so I spoon it into a couple of serving dishes and take it to the table. Rory gestures for me to help myself first. I take a large spoonful of the curry and a smaller helping of the rice. Then Rory plates up his meal and pours two glasses of wine.

It's all so achingly civilized. I have noticed before he has impeccable manners, when he's not being an asshole. We start to eat and Rory murmurs appreciatively. The curry is pretty good.

"What happened earlier should not have happened."

His words catch me so off guard, I just nod in response. I didn't expect him to address that. I imagined he'd be the type to just sweep issues under the rug and forget about them.

"It's okay."

"No, it's not okay. You're my wife now and I scared you. That's unacceptable."

"It's been a shitty day."

"Aye," Rory agrees, "but this curry makes up for it. Where did you learn to cook?"

"From my mom. She was a cook at the school I went to." I take a sip of my wine and set the glass back down. "Do you cook at all?"

"Not really. I can fry an egg, make a decent spaghetti bolognese, but that's about it. We have a housekeeper who does all our cooking."

"Oh, right, Marian." I met her at Libby's wedding. "What about when you're out here? Who cooks for you?"

"We have a woman who takes care of the house and buys our groceries, but if you're wondering who made your breakfast this morning, that was Manus."

"Manus?" I run through the names of all the people I've met since I first started working for Andrew Donovan. "Which one is he?"

"Big brute who trails about after Jacob like a puppy."

Oh, yes. I'd have to be blind not to have noticed him. Manus is built like the proverbial brick shithouse. He's heavily tattooed and an air of menace wafts around him. I'm pretty sure he was at the club when that shit went down.

"Oh, yes. What's his deal?"

"Who knows? He started working for the family when he left school. He ran errands, stuff like that. Then one day he just decided that Jacob needed his protection, and he's stuck to him like glue ever since. It drove my pa crazy, but Manus wouldn't budge. We've all got used to him now."

"So he's a bodyguard?"

Rory nods and shrugs at the same time as if he's not sure that's how he would actually categorize the man.

"And he made those delicious eggs?"

"He did."

"Where did he learn to cook like that?"

"From Marian. He has a bit of a thing for her, but he's too shy to ask her out. It's the family's worst kept secret. He asked her to give him cooking lessons so he could spend time with her."

"And she hasn't realized he likes her?"

"If she has, she's not let on."

There's something very rom com about the situation. It makes me smile. The conversation dies away, but the silence is not uncomfortable. We both eat our dinner and sip our wine, exchanging the occasional glance.

It gives me a chance to think about things. Being pushed into marriage isn't what I wanted, but it doesn't necessarily have to be the end of the world. My life may be able to continue as normal. I decide to test the waters.

"I need to let Andrew know I messed up at the club."

Rory glances up at me. "He knows."

"No, I mean with the countertops for the kitchen. They're the wrong size."

"Is that why you were there so late last night?"

Fuck! Was that only last night? It feels like a lifetime ago.

"Yes. I was trying to work out what went wrong."

Rory puts his fork down. "Your work means a lot to you?"

"Well, yes, but I also don't want to let Andrew down. I don't want to get on his bad side."

"Andrew's not going to hold it against you if you make a mistake, or if there are delays. He's a gruff bastard at times, but he's a businessman. He understands shit happens." Rory drinks some wine and peers at me over the rim of the glass. "Did you think he'd put a hit out on you if you messed up?"

I shrug, because I did sort of think something like that would happen. Rory throws back his head and laughs.

"Oh, sweetheart, it'll be fine. You can sort it out on Thursday when we go back to the city."

"So I can carry on working?"

"Yeah, I'm not some caveman who refuses to let his wife out of the house. You'll have to take a couple of my men with you for safety, but you're free to work or shop, or see your friends, whatever you want."

Why does his reasonable attitude disappoint me? My face falls into a frown.

"What?" Rory says. "Did you think you were a prisoner?"

"No," I lie.

A grin spreads across his face. "Did you want to be a prisoner?"

Even as I shake my head in denial, I realize that there is some part of me that was intrigued by the possibility of being held captive.

Rubbing his chin thoughtfully, Rory studies me. Heat rises to my cheeks and I focus on eating my dinner.

"You want to cede control," Rory says eventually.

"No, I...."

"Yes, you do," he interrupts, cutting off my protest. "All this resistance, denying the spark between us, that was all because you want me to strip away your choices."

"No." I shake my head vehemently. "I don't."

Rory arches an eyebrow at me.

"So, tell me, sweetheart, how did you feel earlier when I spanked you?"

I gnaw on my bottom lip, really not wanting to answer. Rory leans back in his seat, folding his arms across his chest, and says nothing. Eventually, I can't bear the tension that builds and I have to speak.

"It hurt. I was humiliated."

"And?" Rory prompts.

Showing no mercy, he doesn't take his eyes off me. He's going to make me say it.

"I was aroused," I admit.

A wicked grin spreads across Rory's face.

"You were drenched, sweetheart. I knew that wasn't a purely physical response. Your body wanted me, but your mind did, too."

"Perhaps." I spear a piece of broccoli with my fork and stuff it into my mouth, chewing angrily. "So what happens now?"

"Now, we finish our meal, enjoy some ice cream for dessert, and then go upstairs and find out just how much you crave my control."

He flashes me a wink that reminds me of the Irish charmer I first met at a wedding almost a year ago. All objections I harbored melt away. Whatever he wants to do to me, I'm going to let him. The worst of it is I'll probably enjoy every minute of it.

CHAPTER NINE

Rory

GETTING Eleanor to admit she wants me feels like the sweetest victory. A part of me wants to drag her straight upstairs to my room, but now that we've got some of the bullshit out of the way, there's no need to rush.

We finish the incredible meal she cooked and I go to the freezer to search for some ice cream.

"Salted caramel or chocolate cookie crunch?" I ask, holding up two tubs.

"A little of both, please."

"Good choice."

I get a couple of bowls from the cupboard and find an ice cream scoop among the utensils in a drawer by the sink. I serve up our dessert and put the tubs back in the freezer while Eleanor clears the dishes from the table.

"Leave those on the counter," I tell her. "Janice will do them in the morning."

Eleanor hesitates, obviously not liking the idea of leaving work for someone else to do, but as I head back to the table with our ice cream, she follows me.

"How come you got more than me?" she grumbles as she digs her spoon into her bowl.

"Because I'm the man of the house and I'm a sexist pig."

"Are you?"

I was kidding, but Eleanor's question is deadly serious.

"I try not to be, but I guess there are times when I assert my authority." I scoop up some of my ice cream and drop it into her bowl. "But I'm not a tyrant when it comes to sweets."

"Well, thank goodness for that," Eleanor says, "because I don't think I could live with a man who hoards the sugar."

"Oh, believe me, sweetheart, I'll give you all the sugar you can handle."

Eleanor snorts with laughter. There's nothing delicate about the sound. She pours every ounce of mirth she feels into it.

"That was the worst line I've ever heard," she grumbles.

"Give it time. I'm sure I can come up with much worse."

Eleanor smiles and turns her attention to the contents of her bowl. As I eat my own dessert, I watch her licking chocolate ice cream from her spoon.

A deep satisfaction washes over me. Though the way it

happened was not what I would have chosen, I'm pleased this woman is mine now. I am never letting her go.

"You want some coffee?" I ask as she finishes her dessert and drops the spoon into the bowl.

"No, thanks."

"You want to go upstairs?"

She lowers her gaze, suddenly shy. Or is she? Eleanor peeks up at me from beneath thick eyelashes and I see the wicked gleam in her emerald eyes. It seems she wants to play. After all she's been through today, I can give her that.

"Run," I tell her.

"Huh?" she sounds surprised.

"Run."

Catching on, she gets to her feet, gathers her skirts, and runs from the room. Her dress is cumbersome, so I give her a decent head start. It's a mistake. She's faster than I thought and makes it all the way to the front door. She's trying to unlock it when I catch up with her.

Ignoring the twinge in my thigh, I swing her up off her feet and drop her over my shoulder. Taking the stairs two at a time, I carry her to my bedroom, where I set her down in the middle of the floor.

"So this is your lair," she says, taking in the décor.

My room here, like the one in the London house, is decorated in earthy tones. I like a neutral palette.

"It is," I confirm, "and you're trapped here now."

Her eyes gleam. As I suspected, she likes the idea of having her choices taken away.

"Strip," I command. I can't wait to see her gorgeous body.

She reaches behind her and then drops her hands to her sides.

"I said, strip."

She purses her lips. "I can't."

Shit, that's right. She has all those fucking buttons. I go to my nightstand and take a switchblade from the top drawer. Eleanor's eyes widen. The pulse at the base of her throat flickers, perhaps from arousal, definitely from fear. She gasps as I spin her around, pulling her back against me.

"Don't move," I whisper in her ear. "I wouldn't want to cut you by accident."

She doesn't move, barely breathes as I run the blade beneath the top of her dress. I carefully slice down under the buttons until I've opened it enough to be able to tear it off her.

She's left standing there in nothing but those virginal white stockings with the pale pink ribbons securing them in place. Fuck. She looks amazing.

Her hand moves as if to untie the ribbons.

"Leave them on."

She immediately drops her hands to her sides. I like her obedience, but I like the challenge in her eye as she meets my gaze even more.

"Good girl." I believe in giving praise where it's due. "Now, kneel."

Eleanor sinks to the floor. She's naturally graceful and the posture she adopts is perfect. Her spine is straight, her neck long. Her legs are slightly parted, giving me a tantalizing glimpse of her pale pink pussy. She's bare, I notice. I like that.

Her eyes rake over me, lingering, not on my scars like I would have expected, but on the tattoo over my heart. I had it done when I was fifteen and my father officially brought me into the family business. A Celtic cross with our family name etched on it, the tattoo is a badge of honor that all my brothers, cousins and uncles wear. Immense pride surges through me every time I see it.

I shuck off my boxers and my erection springs free. Eleanor gasps but doesn't make some predictable remark about how large my cock is.

"Suck me," I command, "and make it good."

Usually, I'd tell a woman what I like, but I want Eleanor to figure it out for herself. We need to understand each other's bodies if we want to give and receive pleasure.

Eleanor leans forward and tentatively wraps her hand around the base of my cock. Her fingers are freezing, and I try not to react. Where her hands are cold, her mouth is hot. She kisses along the length of my shaft and then places her hands on my butt, pulling me close. She takes a couple of inches of me into her mouth and then draws back a little. Her tongue swirls around my length, running along its underside, tracing the thick blue veins. Her gentle exploration is killing me, but I allow her to take her time, mapping out every inch of me. Then she sucks hard and my control snaps.

Fisting a hand in her hair, I shove my cock to the back of her throat. She chokes and digs her nails into my butt. I pull back a little, allowing her to catch her breath, before driving forward once more. After a couple of thrusts,

Eleanor has tears streaming down her face. Her nostrils flare as she struggles for breath.

"Tap my thigh if you need me to stop."

Though she's clearly struggling, she doesn't give me any sign she wants to stop. I push my cock into her mouth and stroke her cheek.

"Good girl."

As I continue to fuck her mouth, some of the tension drains from her body. I slide back and forth over her gorgeous red lips and she stares up at me. Her hand moves from my butt and she curves it around my balls, squeezing experimentally. I groan as she gets the pressure just right.

"Fuck, your mouth is perfect," I grit out. My balls tighten and I know I'm close. "I'm going to come."

If she tapped out, I would withdraw, but she doesn't, so I hold her head in place as I spill my seed onto her tongue. As I pull out, she swallows every last drop.

"That was fucking incredible," I tell her. "Now it's your turn."

CHAPTER TEN

Eleanor

Rory Donovan is not the first man to use my mouth so ruthlessly, but he is the first who didn't make me feel like it was something sordid. It was the reverence in his gaze that made the difference. He let me know my wellbeing meant something to him and that's why I let him push me beyond my comfort zone.

Putting a hand beneath my elbow, he helps me to my feet. Then he picks me up, bridal style, and carries me to his bed, which is enormous. He tosses me onto the mattress, then grabs my ankles and pulls me to the edge of the bed. My pulse rate picks up as he drops to his knees. I know exactly what he's planning and, as his dark gaze sweeps over me, I just know this is going to be good.

He starts at my ankle, placing soft kisses on the bone. Already, my clit is tingling. Who knew your ankles could be an erogenous zone? Perhaps that's why the Victorians were so obsessed with covering them up. He slowly kisses his way up my leg. He places a hand on my knee and I shriek, instinctively pulling away.

Rory looks up at me, an eyebrow arched, and I giggle. "Sorry, tickly spot."

"Hmm, I'll have to remember that."

Damn, I should have controlled my reactions better. Rory seems like the type who'll torture me mercilessly if he knows I have a weak spot. He carries on his gentle exploration of my body until he reaches my inner thigh. I yelp as he nips the tender flesh with his teeth, then soothes the pain with his tongue. Boy, that feels good.

Putting his palms on my thighs, he spreads me open and lowers his head. I hold my breath as my body thrums with anticipation. I sigh contentedly as he licks along the length of my feminine seam. As the tip of his tongue pushes inside me and swirls around, my eyes roll back in my head. There is no way to describe the sensations coursing through me.

I lift my hips as he laps at my drenched pussy. My clitoris throbs, demanding attention. I wiggle my butt impatiently, and Rory responds, wrapping his lips around the delicate bud and sucking gently. It just about drives me wild with desire.

"Oh, god, Rory!"

I fling my arm across my face, covering my eyes. Rory reaches up and curves a hand around my breast. He draws circles around my nipple with his fingertip and it draws up into a tight peak. Then he pinches it, hard, sending a zap of pain straight to my center. As the pressure builds at my core, I can't hold out any longer. I need him inside me.

"Fuck me!" I demand.

Rory chuckles. "What's the magic word?"

There are so many words I'm tempted to throw at him right now, but I go for the one I know he wants to hear.

"Please."

Rory gets to his feet, flips me over onto my front and pulls me up, so I'm on all fours on the bed. He positions himself behind me and places one hand on my hip to hold me in place. Although I'm wet and ready for him, I still feel a burning sensation as he fills me with his enormous cock. I whimper at the brutal invasion, but he doesn't give me a chance to catch my breath.

He pulls back and then drives into my welcoming body once more. He fucks me at a relentless pace. I try to match his rhythm, but it's impossible. I grab a handful of the sheet below me and hold on tight as he stamps his possession on every inch of me.

Putting his hand on the back of my neck, he pushes me down so my head is on the bed and my bottom is up. At this angle, his cock slides against my clit, making it pulse with desire. I'm close, but not quite there.

"Rory, please," I beg.

"Tell me what you need."

"Touch me."

He slips a hand between my legs and finds my engorged clit. I'm so worked up, the mere touch is enough to take me over the edge. I cry out as my body convulses.

Rory pulls out of me and a moment later, a jet of semen

splatters against the back of my thighs. I look over my shoulder at him.

"That was incredible."

"Aye, sweetheart," he agrees, "it was, but we're not done yet."

Holding a hand out to me, he helps me up off the bed and leads me into his en-suite bathroom. He opens the door to the shower and turns on the water. He puts his hand under the stream to check the temperature and gestures for me to step inside.

I quickly strip off my stockings and get in. Rory immediately follows me, wrapping his arms around my waist as he guides me beneath the water. It's the ideal temperature, hot but not scalding.

I lean back against Rory's chest and sigh. He slides his hand over my abdomen and I part my legs for him. His thumb presses against my clit as he pushes two fingers inside me. He kisses my neck all the way down to my shoulder, then nips me gently. The man has a thing for biting, it seems, and I am here for it.

As he fucks me with his fingers, I tilt my face up toward the water. This is bliss. A moan escapes me as I feel Rory's rock hard cock pressing into my butt.

Withdrawing his fingers, he spins me around and lifts me. I wrap my legs around his waist as he backs me against the tiled wall. He doesn't fuck me at first. He just slides in and out of me at a languorous pace that makes my body thrum with desire.

Then he steps it up, hammering into my helpless body. My head drops back against the wall and I moan as he brings me to the brink once more. His hand cups my butt and he presses a finger against my forbidden hole.

"Has anyone ever fucked you here?" he asks.

"No."

"Good. I want to be the first."

Startled, my eyes drop to his. He chuckles darkly. "But not tonight."

Grateful for that reprieve, I focus on the here and now, enjoying the waves of pleasure washing over me. My pussy clenches around Rory's cock and something inside me detonates.

My hips buck and my mouth twists as I reach my climax. I wrap my arms tight around Rory's neck and hold on as he thrusts up into me three more times before he too reaches his peak. He grunts loudly as his cock jerks. He pulls out of me carefully and strokes my hair. Then he sets me down on my feet, holding onto me until he's sure I'm steady.

"Now," he says, reaching past me to grab a bottle of shampoo, "let's get you cleaned up."

He turns me around and lathers shampoo in my hair. I don't think anyone other than the girl at the hair salon has done this for me since I as a kid. It's so comforting.

Rory takes his time to massage the shampoo into my scalp and wash the thick strands of my hair before helping me to rinse off.

When my hair is done, he takes a bottle of shower gel and pours some into his hand. He cleans every inch of me, slowly, carefully. His touch is gentle, calming rather than arousing, though my clit does pulse when he washes my breasts.

"There," he says, "all done."

I reach for the shower gel, intending to return the favor, but he shakes his head.

"You dry off and get into bed. I'll be there in a minute."

I step out of the shower and pull a fluffy white towel around body. I use another to dry my hair the best I can. It's going to get the pillow wet, but I guess if Rory minded, he'd not have told me to get into the bed.

Once I've dried off thoroughly, I drop the towel into the linen basket behind the bathroom door. Leaving Rory to finish his shower in peace, I get into the bed.

It occurs to me I don't know which side he favors. I've always had a preference for the left, so I get in and hope he's not going to want me to swap.

As I hear the shower switching off, I yawn widely. It's been a hell of a day. I don't think I've ever experienced so many emotional shifts in such a short space of time.

"I wasn't sure which side of the bed you sleep on," I say as Rory comes into the room, still gloriously naked.

"Either's good for me."

He pulls back the sheets and gets into bed. He shuffles closer to me.

"Lie on your side, sweetheart."

I roll onto my side, my back to him, assuming that's what he meant. He wraps an arm around me and drags me a little closer. Who'd have thought Rory Donovan would be a snuggler? More to the point, who'd have thought I would feel so safe in his arms?

Shutting my eyes, I breathe in and out, noting how my chest rises and falls as I slowly drift off to sleep.

CHAPTER ELEVEN

Eleanor

I WAKE with a start as Rory leaps out of bed, cursing violently. Sitting up, I clutch the sheet to my chest and look around to see what's going on.

"Shit!" he swears. "I didn't mean to disturb you."

"That's okay."

I watch him closely. It takes me a moment to realize what's wrong. He's rubbing his thigh and his face is twisted in pain. It looks as if he has cramp.

"Here." I pat the space beside me. "Let me help."

He climbs onto the bed, on top of the sheets, and lies back. I don't really know what I'm doing, but I start to massage his thigh with firm strokes. It's strange after all we did yesterday, but this feels embarrassingly intimate.

"How's that?" I ask. "Too hard?"

"No," he says through gritted teeth. "It's good."

I carry on kneading the muscular flesh. Though I noticed the scar last night, I didn't study it closely. It's a mess. The flesh is puckered and yellow. Whoever tended the wound didn't do a very good job of repairing it. I can't work out what would cause a scar of this shape and size, but I guess whatever it was is the reason for his occasional limp.

"What happened to you?"

"Some asshole shot me."

Stunned by that revelation, I freeze, my hands resting on his leg. I expected him to say he'd been in a car crash. That's the assumption I made when Libby told me he had an injury which caused him pain from time to time. It's a shock to hear him say he was shot.

"Was it, uh…." How do I put this delicately? "Was it a business rival?"

"No, just some petty thug trying to rob me."

That's even more surprising because muggers don't usually run around with guns, not in this country.

"When was this?"

"Uh?" Rory's mouth twists as if he's experiencing another twinge of pain, so I resume massaging his leg. "About two, three years ago."

I can't believe he doesn't know the exact date. If that had happened to me, the precise moment would be etched in my memory. I guess his world is very different from mine.

"And it still hurts?"

I don't know anything about gunshot wounds, but I would have thought he'd have recovered by now.

"There was nerve damage, or something." He shrugs. "I don't know. I never saw a specialist."

"Maybe you should."

Giving me a look that suggests I'm being naïve, Rory shakes his head. "There'd be too many questions."

I nod. A doctor would probably have to report a gunshot wound to the police. I guess Rory and his family use their own people when they get injured.

"What happened to the man who shot you?"

Rory lifts his eyebrows in a manner I'm already familiar with. He's very expressive, saying a lot without even opening his mouth.

"Do you really want to know?"

Do I? Although I wonder how Rory handled the situation, I decide I'm probably better off not knowing what he's capable of. I shake my head.

"That's wise," Rory says. "The less you know about my business, the better."

He's probably right. Although I am curious about what happens in his world, the small glimpse I've had of it is enough for me to realize I can't stomach the violence that comes with being a Donovan. If Rory can shield me from that, it will be easier for me to live with my new situation.

I trail my hand up to caress the scar on the lower right side of his abdomen. It's cleaner than the scar on his thigh. It's surgical, I think.

"What happened here?"

Rory glances down to where my finger is tracing a line along the scar.

"That one's from an operation."

"Appendicitis?" I think the scar is in the right place for that.

"No." Rory lets out a long, slow exhale. "My mother was sick. I gave her one of my kidneys."

My jaw drops. "What?"

Rory shrugs, like it's no big deal.

"She was sick for a long time. When her kidneys began to fail, the whole family got tested. I was a match."

"So you gave up a kidney?"

Rory pushes himself into a seated position. His labored breathing tells me it was a struggle for him. I don't like that he's in pain. He leans back against the headboard.

"Don't make me out to be a hero," he says. "I did what any man would do."

I'm not sure that's true.

"Well, I think it's pretty incredible."

"So, what, you like me now that you know I donated a kidney?"

I shake my head sadly. "Liking you has never been the issue, Rory." Although I've always been wary of him, I have found him to be charming and sexy at times. It's what he represents I disapprove of. "Your family, what you do, it scares me."

"Technically, I'm the family accountant, if that makes it less scary."

"Accountant?" I scoff, assuming that's some sort of euphemism for bookie or money launderer. "Can you tell me, hand on heart, that you sit in an office all day and crunch numbers, that you've never beaten someone up, or worse?"

He takes a deep breath and scrubs a hand over his face. "No, I can't tell you that."

"I thought not."

Rory reaches over and takes my hand.

"Look, sweetheart, I know you're having trouble accepting our situation, but it is what it is and there's nothing I either of us can do to change it."

I consider baiting him with the possibility I could go to the police and tell them I've been coerced into marrying him because of an incident I witnessed. Imagining how Rory would react to that, I decide not to disturb that particular hornet's nest.

"Okay, I guess I'll have to live with it." A thought crosses my mind, something I hadn't considered about my new status as mob wife. "Shit! I'm going to have to tell my mother I'm married."

"Aye," Rory agrees, "I suppose you will. Do you want to call her?"

Though I am tempted to break the news to my mother that I've married a man she's never even heard of over the phone, I can't do it. We don't see each other as often as we'd like, but my mother and I have a good relationship.

"I'd rather tell her face to face. Can we go see her sometime?"

"Okay," Rory agrees easily. "We can do it today, if you like."

"Today?"

"No time like the present."

I'm taken aback by his enthusiasm for the idea. He looks at me, expectation etched on his face, as I try to decide whether to take him up on the offer.

It's so sudden. I need time to think of a story to tell my mother. Then I realize the longer I leave it, the worse it will be. If I wait three months to break the news, she's going to wonder why I tried to hide it for so long.

"Okay, I'd like that."

"Good. We can visit your mom and then go shopping."

"Shopping?"

"Aye, you'll need a new dress for Andrew's birthday dinner."

I wave a hand dismissively. "No, it's fine. I have something at home that will do."

Rory shakes his head, an indulgent smile playing on his lips. "No offense, sweetheart, but I've seen your idea of a party dress. Take it from me, you need something new."

I could waste energy being offended that he thinks my clothes aren't good enough, but he's right. My wardrobe largely consists of work wear. Having seen how Libby and Sorcha dress, even on a day-to-day basis, I know nothing I possess is going to measure up.

"I assume you're buying."

"Of course. You're my wife. I want to spoil you."

"Well, okay," I tell him. "Just this once I want to let you."

"Right, then." Rory gets up from the bed, his movement less stiff than it was. "You grab a shower and I'll rustle up some breakfast. I'd like to get to Canterbury by ten, so we have plenty of time to visit with your mom before we hit the clothes stores."

There's no point in pretending I'm surprised he knows where my mother lives. Though I'm sure he's dug into my background, it would be a simple case of asking Libby about my family. She knows my mother raised me by herself and that she moved to Kent after I left school and she had no need to work there anymore.

I get up and walk to the bathroom, not caring that I'm completely naked. Rory's seen my body from several different angles now, so shyness is unnecessary.

As I reach the door, I look back at my husband, who's eyeing me appreciatively.

"My mother's a good woman," I say. "But she's never had the life she deserves. She's had to work hard for everything she owns."

Though I'm not ashamed of my humble background, I can't bear the thought of Rory looking at my mother's rundown home, her thrift store clothing and judging her against his own wealthy family.

Rory nods. "I understand, sweetheart. You have nothing to worry about."

As I turn and head for the shower, I can't help thinking, "if only that was true."

CHAPTER TWELVE

Rory

Eleanor frets for almost the entire drive from the mansion to her mother's house. She tells me repeatedly that the house is small, that a lot of the furniture was bought secondhand. She needn't worry about me looking down on her mother. My own family came from humble beginnings.

When we moved to London at first, my father worked for a minor gangster, running errands and shaking down small business owners for protection money. We lived in a poky apartment over a betting shop. Ciaran, Aidan and I had to share a bedroom, while my parents slept on a pull-out sofa in the living room.

It took years for my father to work his way up through the ranks, but by the time Jacob came along, he'd formed his own organization and the money was pouring in.

I guess that's what separates me and Aidan from our younger brothers. They were born into privilege while we had to struggle for every morsel of food we ate.

It's why they prefer to focus on our legitimate income streams, I think. They didn't receive the same baptism of fire that the rest of us did.

When we get to the street where her mother lives, the tension thrumming through Eleanor's veins becomes palpable. My Range Rover stands out against the rusted up cars parked outside the terraced houses.

"It's that one, there." Eleanor points to number seventy-three.

I pull up at a house with a neat garden at the front. It's better cared for than the ones on either side. There's gravel, rather than grass, but there are still plenty of vibrant flowers in pots dotted around the small space.

Hanging baskets frame the front door. I can't help noticing the doorstep is freshly painted in a bright red color. Eleanor's mother may not have much, but she takes care of what she's got.

Turning off the engine, I get out of the car. Eleanor doesn't wait for me to help her. She gets out of her side and comes to join me on the narrow sidewalk.

"It's going to be fine," I assure her, grabbing her hand and entwining my fingers with her.

Eleanor nods. We walk to the front door and she rings the bell. That surprises me. I thought she'd have a key.

A few seconds pass before a woman answers the door. She's a couple of inches shorter than Eleanor, with graying brown hair. She's older than I thought she'd be, in her late fifties, perhaps.

Dressed in a long floral skirt and a white top, she wears a simple gold chain with a heart-shaped pendant around her neck.

"Ellie, what are you doing here?" she asks as she throws her arms around her daughter and hugs her.

Ellie? I like that. It's less formal than Eleanor.

"Just thought we'd pop in and surprise you," Eleanor says.

Eleanor's mother turns her attention to me.

"And who is this?"

"Uh, this is Rory Donovan." She waves a hand between me and her mother, her nervousness permeating the air. "Rory, this is my mom, eh, Anne Finlay."

"Annie," her mother says, accepting the hand I offer her and shaking it firmly.

"Nice to meet you, Annie." I offer her my best son-in-law smile, something I've had no practice of, and wink cheekily as she steps aside to let us into the house.

We walk straight into a small living room. It's cozy, with a couple of armchairs and a sofa, all in a dark brown fabric. There's a low glass-topped coffee table at the center of the seating configuration.

The floor is covered with an engineered hardwood and the walls are painted in a warm shade of cream. It's homely.

There's a bookcase with some books on it, but its shelves are mainly filled with ornaments and photos of Eleanor at various stages of her school career. I'll need to get a closer look at those later.

"Mum, I've got some news," Eleanor says, a slight

tremble in her voice. I squeeze her hand to offer reassurance.

Annie's eyes drop to my wife's stomach. Shit. It would be too soon for a pregnancy, but I hadn't even considered protection yesterday. I have no clue if Eleanor is on any form of birth control. My hand tightens around hers.

"I'm not pregnant, mom. I'm careful, you know that."

Her words are probably as much for me as they were for her mother. I relax a little.

Though the idea of Eleanor carrying my child sparks some primal sense of satisfaction in me, we are nowhere near ready to think about babies.

She's had enough thrust upon her without having to bear a child she's not ready for.

"That's good," her mother murmurs approvingly. "So what's your news?"

Eleanor holds out her left hand to show off her rings. "Rory and I got married."

Her mother's eyes widen, and she sinks onto the arm of the nearest chair.

"When?"

"Uh, yesterday."

She scrunches up her nose as she looks at Eleanor. "You got married on a Tuesday?"

That's what she's surprised about? I have to hold back a laugh.

"Yes, it was a spur-of-the-moment thing. It was just me, Rory, and our witnesses. It wasn't a big deal."

Her mother tuts. "Marriage is a big deal, Eleanor."

"I know. That's not what I meant."

"I know what you meant." Her mother narrows her

eyes on me as her expression turns to one of suspicion. "How can you get married on the spur of the moment? There's paperwork to fill in. Is your marriage even legal?"

"It's legal," I assure her. "I have a few connections, so I was able to pull some strings and expedite the paperwork."

In truth, it was Aidan who got that side of things organized. I'd been too shell-shocked by his ultimatum to deal with the legal aspects of my marriage to Eleanor.

"Well," Annie gets to her feet. "I can't say I'm not disappointed you didn't introduce Rory to me until now, but if you're happy, Ellie, then so am I."

"I am happy!"

Eleanor lets go of my hand and goes to hug her mother once more. When she steps back, there's a very convincing smile on her face. If I didn't know better, I'd think she was ecstatic about becoming my wife.

On the way here, I didn't warn her not to alert her mother to how the marriage really came about, but I knew I wouldn't have to. Eleanor's response to the whole situation has shown her pragmatic side. She isn't going to risk her mother's safety or her own by saying something stupid.

"Then I'm glad for you," Annie says, "but I am a bit disappointed I couldn't be there. You know, I always dreamed of giving you away."

Eleanor grimaces. "Sorry, we just got swept up in the romance of it. We're planning another ceremony later in the year so everyone can come."

I'm stunned that she suggested what I was about to.

Mollified, her mother smiles. "That sounds wonderful.

Now, how about some tea? I've got a batch of muffins fresh out of the oven this morning."

"What kind of muffins?" I ask.

"Lemon and poppy seed."

I have something of a sweet tooth.

"Sounds good."

Annie gestures toward the sofa. "Well, make yourselves comfortable and I'll be back in a minute."

I lead Eleanor to the sofa and let go of her hand as she sits. I wander over to the bookcase to examine the school photos more closely.

They're all posed in a similar fashion, with Eleanor facing the camera at a sideways angle. There's a pale blue backdrop in each of them. Her uniform comprises a black blazer, shirt, and tie.

She was a pretty child, which is unsurprising since she's such a beautiful young woman. It saddens me, though, that her smile looks forced in the images. It doesn't reach her eyes.

"I hated school," Eleanor says, coming up behind me and putting a hand on my shoulder. "People were so cruel."

"Libby mentioned something about that."

Eleanor nods. "She was one of the rich, popular kids. She wasn't as bad as most, but she could be mean when she wanted to be."

I put the photo I was holding down and turn to Eleanor. "Libby bullied you?"

"Yeah, but we've put that behind us. She got a taste of what it was like to be mocked and ignored after that scandal with her dad. It taught her a lesson, I guess."

"But you're friends now?"

"We're friendly." Eleanor looks off to the side as she considers that for a moment. "Yes, we're friends."

I'm glad to hear it. Our family spends a lot of time together and Eleanor will need to find a way to fit in. Her friendship with Libby will help, and I know Sorcha has a soft spot for her. Aidan's wife, Madeline, is the unknown quantity. She can be a real bitch when she wants to be, especially when she's unhappy.

I turn back to the display of photographs and something catches my eye, a silver trophy, shaped like an artist's palette. Picking it up carefully, I read the inscription.

"First place in the Gray's School of Art Junior competition." I look at Eleanor. "What is this?"

"It was a competition I won in my final year at school. Grays is a prestigious art school in Scotland. It was an honor to win it."

There's a hint of longing in her voice that I can't help but notice.

"You didn't pursue art?"

"Couldn't afford it. I needed to find a job straight after school and when nothing came up, I decided to use my talents in a practical way, so I started doing interior design jobs. Andrew is the first big client I've had."

"You can afford it now," I tell her. "If you want to go to art school, we can make it happen."

"Yeah, maybe." She sounds less enthusiastic than I thought she would. Then she smiles. "Yeah, I'll look into it."

Putting her trophy back on the shelf, I follow Eleanor

over to the sofa and sit next to her as Annie comes back into the room and sets a tray down on the coffee table.

"How do you take your tea, Rory?"

I don't have the heart to tell her I never touch the stuff, so I just ask for it without milk or sugar. She pours me a cup and hands me a small plate, indicating I should help myself to a muffin.

"These look incredible," I tell her and she beams widely.

Eleanor pours her own tea and grabs a muffin. As her mother sits down, she glances at me.

"Donovan? Didn't Liberty Preston marry a Donovan?"

"Yes," Eleanor confirms. "That's where I met Rory, at their wedding. Libby married his brother."

"Oh, right. Doesn't Libby's husband run nightclubs?"

The pursing of her lips tells me Annie doesn't approve of that.

"He does," I confirm.

"And what do you do, Rory?"

"Rory's an accountant," Eleanor replies on my behalf. "He looks after his family's finances."

That seems more to Annie's liking. "So you've a good head on your shoulders, then. I'm glad to hear my Ellie's in safe hands."

"The safest," I assure her. "I will never let anything bad happen to your daughter."

Though the words are intended to reassure Annie, I mean them. Eleanor is mine now and I will protect her to my last breath.

CHAPTER THIRTEEN

Eleanor

As we pull away from my mother's house, I lean my head back against the car seat and let out a long, slow sigh of relief. That went so much better than I expected.

I've only brought a boyfriend home to meet my mom once before, and she hated him on sight. Granted, he was a cocky asshole with no real achievements to back up his arrogant attitude. She didn't hold back on letting him know exactly what she thought of him.

Despite her initial shock when I introduced Rory as my husband, she warmed to him quickly. It's not surprising. When he turns on the charm, he's hard to resist.

"Thanks for being so nice to my mom."

"It wasn't a chore," Rory says. "She's a great lady."

"Yes, she is." Dropping my gaze to my wedding ring, I twist it around on my finger. "Look, I'm sorry I blurted out that thing about us having another wedding. It's just, she was disappointed to have missed out and I wanted to give her something to look forward to."

"It's fine," Rory assures me.

"I mean, we can tell her in a few weeks that we changed our minds."

Rory tuts at me. "We can't do that. She's already planning what she'll wear."'

"I know, but…"

"But, nothing," Rory interjects. "I want to do the whole thing again, the way you want to this time."

I arch an eyebrow, because even if I plan the whole thing, it's still going to be the result of an ultimatum I was given.

"Really? Can I swap the groom for someone of my choosing?"

"No." Rory doesn't take the bait. "But you can pick a venue, and a cake and bridesmaids, and all that shit."

"But it still won't be a real wedding."

Rory shoots me a dark glare. "It will be a real wedding. Our marriage is real, Eleanor, whether you accept that, or not."

My lip wobbles, and he sighs.

"Anyway, by the time the wedding comes around, you'll be head over heels in love with me."

"Arrogant swine!" I say with a laugh, thought I fear he might be right. Falling for him wouldn't be difficult. He is a charming rogue when he wants to be. Life would certainly be easier if I did give love a chance to blossom. I don't want to think about that right now, though.

"So, where are we headed?"

Rory shrugs. "Where do you usually shop?"

I name a couple of high street stores and even before he shakes his head, I know they're not what he had in mind. He takes his cellphone from his jacket pocket and hands it to me.

"Call Sorcha. She'll tell you where we should go."

"Okay, what's the passcode?"

"2-8-0-4."

I wonder what the significance of the number is. Rory must read my mind.

"It's my mother's birthday."

He clearly loved his mother deeply which I guess is another point in his favor. Damn. I don't want to see all the good in him, not when I'm still mad about being pushed into marrying him.

I enter the code into his phone and find his list of contacts. There are hundreds of them. Does he really know all these people?

I have six names on my phone and two of them are for paint suppliers. I scroll down until I find Sorcha's name and press the button to call her.

"Rory Donovan," she answers after a couple of seconds. "What have you done now?"

I grin, liking her feistiness.

"It's not Rory, it's Eleanor."

"Oh, hi, are you okay? Did you stab him in his sleep? Do you need a clean-up crew, some cash, a passport?"

"Couldn't you have offered me those things before I married him?"

Rory slants a look of disapproval at me. He clearly

doesn't like how this conversation is going. I clear my throat.

"Uh, I need a new dress. Rory told me to ask you where would be a good place to shop."

"That depends. Is it your money or his?"

"His money."

"In that case, your best bet is Harrods. You can get everything you need there. Tell Rory I'll call and arrange a personal shopper for you."

"Oh, okay." I end the call and hand Rory his phone back.

"Well, where did she suggest?"

I grimace because I'd have chosen somewhere less fancy.

"Harrods. She's going to phone ahead and get us a personal shopper."

"Ah, good idea. I should have thought of that myself."

I'm glad he doesn't seem outraged by the suggestion we shop at one of London's most exclusive stores, but I'm not sure I like the idea of spending a lot of his money.

"Isn't it a bit pricey?"

Rory shakes his head. "For my wife, no."

I don't argue but, for the rest of the drive back to the city, I'm quiet. It just seems wrong to let Rory take me shopping when I'm still wondering if there's a way out of this marriage.

In the end, I decide to just let him buy me a new dress. May as well enjoy the perks of being a mob wife.

When we get to the store, Rory parks on the street outside. I'm not sure it's legal to leave a car here, but he doesn't give a shit. He jumps out and, as always, comes to help me out.

Putting an arm around my waist, his hand resting on my hip in a proprietorial manner, Rory steers me into the store. As we pass the liveried doorman, I feel scruffy in my blue jeans and the white blouse I bought from the clothing section in my local grocery store.

When I packed my bag, I grabbed comfortable clothing for a life on the run. I didn't plan for something like this and I feel about of place.

Rory, on the other hand, gives no indication of possessing an inferiority complex. Why would he? His suit is custom made to show off his impressive frame to perfection. His shoes are of the finest Italian leather. I hate to think what the watch on his wrist cost, but I'm willing to bet it was more than his car.

We're walking toward the escalators when a woman approaches. She's a petite brunette, with a slim figure and a warm smile.

"Hello, Mr. and Mrs. Donovan?" she asks. "The other Mrs. Donovan said you'd be coming by. I'm Rachel and I'm here to assist you with whatever you need."

Though her manner is friendly and professional, I detect a hint of nervousness in her voice. I guess she knows who the Donovans are.

"Thanks, Rachel," I give her a smile that I hope will help her feel more at ease. "I need a nice dress for a family dinner."

Rory shakes his head. "She needs a new wardrobe, everything from lingerie to an overcoat." He leans down and whispers in my ear. "Don't argue."

"Wouldn't dream of it," I mutter as Rachel makes notes on her iPad.

"Right this way," Rachel says, walking ahead of us.

I glower at Rory. "If you want to waste money on your fake wife, who am I to stop you?"

I regret my words the minute I say them. Rory tightens his grip on me.

"Watch yourself, Eleanor," he warns. "Don't be foolish enough to imagine I won't punish you in a public place."

I open my mouth to offer some retort, and then snap it shut. Why am I trying to pick a fight with him. Antagonizing him doesn't help my situation and, besides, it's not five minutes since I decided I should just go with the flow and accept whatever he wanted to buy for me.

"I'm sorry," I whisper as we follow Rachel through the store to the elevators.

Rory doesn't respond. He pulls me into the elevator. We ascend in silence, emerging into what looks like a hotel lobby, with tables and chairs dotted around. There are several other customers here.

"Can we offer you some refreshments?" Rachel asks,

"We'll take some sparkling water," Rory replies on my behalf.

"Uh, still for me," I interject. "I don't like sparkling."

"Okay," Rachel says, "Why don't you take a seat while I gather a few things for you to try on?"

"Thank you."

As she walks off, I take a seat on one of the high-backed armchairs. Rory sits opposite me.

"This place is nice," I say, trying to break the tension

between us. "I hope Rachel can find something suitable for tomorrow night."

"She will," Rory replies. "It's what she's paid to do."

"Should we get Andrew a present while we're here?"

"No, I already got him a watch and a bottle of Balvenie Portwood."

I don't know what that is but I'm guessing it's an expensive whisky since Libby said that was one of the things he likes.

Silence descends between us. I'm not sure if Rory is angry or hurt. Perhaps it's a bit of both. I wasn't exactly grateful that he plans to buy me a whole new set of clothes.

As he takes out his cellphone and scrolls through his messages, I pick up the magazine lying on the table in front of me and read a couple of articles.

After fifteen minutes or so of learning about some of the hottest new restaurants in town, I come to a review of the first club I designed for Andrew.

"Hey, look." I hold the magazine up to show Rory. "There's a piece about Sadie's West 55 in here. They loved it."

"Of course they did," Rory says. "You did an amazing job on the design."

"You designed Sadies?" I glance up as Rachel speaks. I hadn't noticed her returning to us. "I've tried to get in there, but it's impossible."

"What have you got for us?" Rory asks impatiently. I'll bet he thought she was angling for us to get her entry to the club.

Rachel clears her throat as her cheeks redden. "I have

several options for Mrs. Donovan to try." She turns to me. "Please follow me to your private dressing room."

She leads the way into a room with a sofa, a table with a couple of glasses and two bottles of water on it, and a changing area, separated by a curtain.

Rory takes a seat on the sofa and Rachel shows me the various items of clothing she's picked out. Everything is so pretty.

"Try that green dress first," Rory says.

Rachel takes it off the rack and hands it to me. As I step into the changing area, I hear Rory dismissing her.

I slip off my own clothes and pull the dress on over my head. It's stunning. I love the way it hugs my waistline and then flares out over my hips. It gives me a more impressive ass than the one I have.

When I step out to show Rory, he nods.

"That's perfect for a family dinner."

Well, that was easy. I gesture toward the rack of clothing. "Should I try anything else on?"

"Aye, that cream one."

I grab it off the rail and take it into the changing area. I've no sooner got it on, than Rory opens the curtain and crowds into my space.

"What do you think of this one?" I ask. "I like it too."

"I don't give a fuck about the dress."

His intent is clear in the dark gleam in his eye. I put my hand on his chest and try to shove him away but, of course, he's immovable.

"Rory," I warn. "We can't have sex in here. It's tacky."

"Who said anything about sex?"

He grabs my shoulders and spins me around, plastering me against the wall. He hikes my skirt up and rips my white lace panties right off me.

"I'm going to fuck you."

Immediately, wetness pools between my legs. I wiggle my hips impatiently as Rory unbuckles his belt, lowers his pants, and pulls down his boxer shorts.

Already fully erect, he positions himself behind me and kicks my feet apart. He pulls my hips back until I'm just where he wants me. His hand slaps across my mouth as he leans forward to whisper in my ear.

"You're mine, Eleanor. Wherever, whenever I want you, you are mine."

That should not turn me on, but it does. My clit throbs as excitement courses through my veins.

"Mmm-hmm," I murmur my agreement behind his hand.

He pumps his hips forcefully, pushing me up onto my toes. This isn't going to be gentle. He fucks me with ruthless determination, smothering my moans with his hand.

"This is for me," he says. "You don't get to come."

So this is a punishment for what I said earlier. I whimper and press my hips back to meet his thrusts. I wiggle my butt, trying to get him to relent as he mercilessly uses my body for his own pleasure.

He responds by spanking my ass twice. It hurts less than the ruler did creating a warmth that spreads deep inside me, taking me closer to ecstasy.

Pressure builds at my core. I'm close, but I can't catch the high I'm looking for. Rory rotates his hips, taking me to the brink.

"If you come, I'll thrash your ass raw."

Despite the threat, I struggle to hold off my orgasm. I have no idea how I manage, but as Rory grunts and finishes inside me I haven't climaxed. He pulls out of my body, leaving me a sticky, unfulfilled mess.

"Let that be a lesson to you," he says as he throws back the curtain and walks back out into the main room. "Only good girls receive pleasure from me."

As he goes and retakes his seat on the sofa, I bow my head. Lesson learned. I won't act like an ungrateful brat again.

CHAPTER FOURTEEN

Rory

FAMILY DINNERS at my house are always a boisterous affair. We're a loud and demonstrative bunch and I'm not sure how Eleanor's going to cope since she's not got no siblings of her own.

I wrap an arm around her waist as we go in through the front door. It's partly because I want to give her a sense of security and partly because I think she'd run if I gave her the chance.

We step into the hallway and voices drift along the corridor from the dining room. The first people we encounter are Sorcha and her kids. She's in the living room, reading my niece and nephew a bedtime story. As we enter, she gets to her feet.

"Eleanor!" she exclaims. "You look fantastic."

My chest swells with pride. My wife is gorgeous

tonight in the green dress I bought her yesterday, along with a whole wardrobe of clothes and shoes, including the impossibly high heels she's wearing.

At my insistence, she left her hair loose. It tumbles in soft curls down over her shoulders. Pre-Raphaelite paintings can't compare to her beauty.

Sorcha is also dressed to the nines, as usual. She's a stunning woman, but tonight she looks tired. She was widowed far too young. I can't help thinking she should be out having fun. She should be dating someone new by now, but Aidan seems to want her locked away here forever, remaining faithful to our brother's memory.

"These are my children," Sorcha says, pulling me from my thoughts. "Donal and Cora, this is Eleanor."

Three-year-old Cora smiles shyly and hides behind her mother's legs. With her blonde curls and pale skin, she looks like a little cherub. She's a sweetheart most of the time, but there are moments when she displays the legendary Donovan temper.

Donal, ever-protective of his mum, steps in front of her. At almost five, he's already showing signs of being his father's son. He scowls at Eleanor.

"Who's she?" he demands.

"Your ma told you, she's Eleanor," I tell him. "She's my wife."

"You don't have a wife." His tone is petulant.

"He does now," Sorcha says in that quiet but firm tone she uses with her kids. "And you'd better be nice to her."

Donal continues to glare at Eleanor, a wonderful welcome to the family. I'm tempted to reprimand the little shit, but I don't like to step on Sorcha's toes. Aidan has no such issue. With Ciaran gone, he has no qualms about exerting his authority. He's grooming the boy to take our older brother's place one day.

"You forgot the bag," Eleanor says suddenly and I realize I left Andrew's gifts and the toys we brought for the kids, in the car.

"I'll go get it."

Kissing her cheek, I head back out to the car, just as Jacob's car pulls up, the ever-present Manus at the wheel. Jacob gets out of the car and storms into the house, muttering furiously. If he sees me, he gives no indication of it.

"What's wrong with him?" I ask Manus as he gets out of the car.

"Woman trouble."

"What woman?"

"The one Aidan dumped on him."

Ah, the heiress Jacob mentioned.

"Word to the wise, Rory," Manus says. "Don't tease him about her. He's not in the mood."

"Fair enough," I say, though I'm now intrigued by the effect this unknown woman has had on Jacob. "I'll leave him be."

Manus nods and walks off around the side of the house. He always uses the back door. I don't know how many times we've invited him to come in the front way, or to join us for dinner, but he always refuses. It's crazy because at this point he's practically family, to my younger brother, at least.

I get the bag from the back of the car and return to the house. Sorcha and Eleanor are laughing about something.

It pleases me they're getting along. The kids, however, seem to be frozen exactly as I left them.

I hold the bag out to Eleanor. She reaches inside to retrieve the toys we brought. There's a fluffy brown bear for Cora and a gray dinosaur for Donal that has to be the ugliest thing I've ever seen. Eleanor was sure he'd love it, though, and it seems she was right.

As she holds the toys out for the kids, they race over and practically snatch them out of their hands. Fuck. Why have I never noticed what ill-mannered little monsters they are? Probably because I was never hoping to make a good impression on a woman before.

Sorcha rolls her eyes despairingly as her kids retreat to her side.

"What do you say to Auntie Eleanor?" she asks.

"Thank you, Auntie Eleanor" they chorus.

That's better, I guess.

"Okay," Sorcha says, "now head upstairs to Lisa. It's time for bed."

Predictably, there are moans and groans. No doubt sensing a party is about to get underway, the kids don't want to miss out.

Leaving Sorcha to deal with their nonsense, I steer Eleanor through to the dining room. Aidan and Jacob are standing by the drinks table, obviously arguing. Andrew and Libby are at the other side of the room, whispering quietly to one another. She's wearing a gold mini dress that makes me think they're planning to hit a club after dinner.

I clear my throat loudly, getting everyone's attention.

"Everyone, you remember Eleanor, my wife. Eleanor, I think you know everyone."

"Uh, yes," she says shyly, "hi."

As a murmur of greetings goes around the room, Eleanor stares at the floor. I worried she'd be overwhelmed and I may be right. Thankfully, Libby comes over to embrace her.

"You look great," Libby says.

"So do you." Eleanor returns the compliment.

"We're going to the new club later. Andrew can't stay away from the place. He loves everything you did."

Eleanor blushes. She seems to have trouble accepting compliments. Sorcha joins us at that moment, sparing my wife the need to come up with a response.

"I'm sorry, Eleanor," Sorcha says. "The kids aren't always so rude."

"They were just shy." Eleanor is more generous than I would be. "Don't worry about it."

Sorcha and Libby both send pointed looks in my direction, and I realize they want Eleanor to themselves. I don't warn her to watch what she says. Within these walls, it doesn't matter, and I trust her to behave.

"I'll leave you ladies to catch up."

I walk off, heading for Aidan and Jacob first. They stop bickering as I approach.

"Whatever's going on with you two, park it for tonight," I warn them.

Aidan's jaw clenches, but after a couple of beats, he nods. He doesn't let many people get away with telling him what to do, but we've stood by each other's sides since we were kids, and I have more leeway than most.

When Jacob doesn't respond, I smack his arm.

"Yes, okay," he agrees, rubbing his arm as if I actually hurt him.

Sensing that hostilities have ceased, Andrew saunters over. I pass him the bag.

"Happy birthday, kid."

"Thanks, Rory."

He pulls the bottle of whisky out of the bag first.

Aidan whistles appreciatively. "Nice."

"We'll open it after dinner," Andrew says. "I'll need a stiff drink. Libby's dragging me to the club again."

"Funny, she said you were the one who wants to spend all his time there."

"Hah. The perils of having a twenty-one-year-old wife. Just wait until Eleanor starts dragging you out every night."

Shit. Realizing Eleanor is the same age as my younger brother's wife is startling. I don't want to think about it.

"Open your other present," I tell him.

He reaches into the bag again and takes out the box, which contains the Hublot Classic Titanium watch I bought him. He opens it and shakes his head before throwing his arms around me in a manly hug.

"It's great. Thanks, man."

"Anything for my third favorite brother."

He snorts derisively and quickly puts on the watch, before hurrying over to show Libby.

"How's it going with your new bride?" Aidan asks me. "Not giving you any problems, I trust."

"Nope." She's giving me plenty, but it's none of his

business. I can't resist getting a dig in at him. "Where's the lovely Madeline tonight?"

His jaw clenches.

"She has a migraine."

"Really?" Jacob sends him a filthy look. "You sure it's not a two hundred pound pain in her ass?"

"What the fuck did you say?" Aidan snarls.

"Exactly what I'd have said if he didn't get there first." I put my arm around Aidan's shoulder and pull him away from our younger brother before they come to blows. I lead him out into the corridor. "Calm the fuck down, Aidan."

His nostrils flare in irritation.

"The little shit winds me up sometimes."

"Yeah, well, you're pretty easy to wind up. Let him take a shot at you. He's obviously pissed at you right now."

Aidan scrubs a hand over his face. "Yeah, 'cause I've done the dirty on him by handing him a beautiful woman who's about to take over a billion pound organization. What a bastard I am."

"Nobody likes interference, Aidan."

He gives me a speculative look. "You talking about him, or you?"

"Both. I think this thing with Eleanor might work out okay, but I don't like how it came about."

"Well, what was I supposed to do with the girl? Would you have preferred I slit her throat and dumped her in the Thames?"

Anger courses through me and I clench my fists at my sides before I'm tempted to land a blow on him.

"No, but let me ask you this. How did you decide

Andrew's club was an appropriate venue to off a guy the night she was working late? It's not a coincidence, is it?"

Guilt crosses his face, and I have my answer.

"I thought so, you fucking asshole. Now, let's go back in there, put our shit aside for now, and celebrate our wee brother's thirtieth."

Aidan shakes his head. "It's not his thirtieth."

"Isn't it?" I could have sworn this was the year.

"No, he's like twenty-eight."

"Fuck. That watch was ten grand."

"Aye, and now you'll have to top it when he does turn thirty."

Oh, well, it's a good thing I love my brother. Aidan and I return to the dining room, just as Marian brings in the first course.

My oldest brother sits at the head of the table as usual. I take the seat to his right, and Eleanor sits next to me. Andrew, Libby and Sorcha sit opposite us and Jacob takes up his position beside Eleanor.

Marian and Rosalyn, her assistant, serve up a chicken liver parfait with an onion jam and little crispbreads. It looks delicious but, before we can eat, Aidan taps his glass to get our attention.

"I'd like to propose a toast, to Andrew on his birthday."

We all raise the glasses of wine someone must have poured while Aidan and I were out of the room.

"To Andrew."

"And," Aidan continues, "I'd like to take a moment to welcome Eleanor to the family. You're one of us now. May you live a long and happy life with my brother."

There's an implicit threat in his words. Eleanor stiffens beside me and blushes deeply when everyone toasts her.

"Are you okay?" I ask as we start eating.

"Fine." There's a quiver in her voice that tells me she caught the warning Aidan issued. She pops a forkful of the parfait into her mouth and swallows it down. "This is delicious."

"Marian is the best cook," Libby says. "You are going to love living here."

"What?" Eleanor turns to me, eyebrows drawn down into a deep frown.

I haven't had the chance to explain our new living arrangements to her yet. I don't know what she expected but for the sake of security the family lives under one roof, well, two, since we also have the mansion in the countryside. We all have private accommodation here, as well as several communal spaces we share.

Jacob also has an apartment of his own in Kensington. He bought it as an investment years ago. He stays there when the family business gets too much for him, or when he's entertaining some lassie he doesn't want the rest of us to meet. Aidan allows it because Manus stays there with him.

"That reminds me," Sorcha says before I can reply to Eleanor. "Your things arrived from your old place this afternoon. I hope you don't mind, but I had Rosalyn unpack everything. She left the boxes with your photos and personal papers for you to sort through."

"Uh, yeah, that's fine," Eleanor says, politeness overriding whatever outrage she feels. "Thank you."

She doesn't speak to me for the rest of the meal and I

know she's pissed when she can't even raise a smile for the chocolate caterpillar cake Marian brings in for Andrew. It's a tradition that each of us gets the same cake for every birthday. We've had the same one since we were kids.

Unfortunately, I'm not the only one who notices her sullenness. When Eleanor goes off with Libby and Sorcha to have coffee in the living room, without so much as a word, Aidan fixes his attention on me.

"Does your new bride have a problem?"

"Nothing I can't handle it."

"Then handle it. You cannot let her disrespect you like that."

"Leave her alone," Andrew says, handing Aidan a glass of the whisky I bought him. "She's shy, and this is overwhelming for her."

I'm grateful for his intervention, but Aidan persists.

"Shy is one thing, sulky is another. Get her under control, or I will."

"The fuck you will."

Aidan leans back in his seat. "Try me."

I suspect with Madeline giving him a hard time, he's looking for someone to take it out on but I am not going to let that person be Eleanor.

I grab the glass Andrew holds out to me and knock the whisky back in one go, a travesty since it deserved to be savored. Pushing to my feet, I jab a finger at Aidan.

"You leave Eleanor the fuck alone. I will deal with her."

I march through to the living room, grab a startled Eleanor by the wrist and drag her upstairs to what is now our bedroom. When I close the door behind us, she pulls her arm free of my grip.

"What the hell are you doing?" she demands.

"What did I say to you about acting like a brat?"

She puts her hands on her hips. "What did I do?"

"Downstairs at dinner, the silent treatment."

"You deserved that."

"Why? Because I forgot to mention we'd be living here?"

"It's a kind of important thing to forget to tell me about."

Fire flashes in her eyes. She's bristling with outrage and I am so turned on right now. Grabbing her by the shoulders, I claim her mouth in a brutal kiss. She pushes against my chest, breaking free of my grasp.

Before I know wha's happening, she draws her arm back and slaps me hard, across the face. Paralyzed by shock, I don't react when Eleanor grabs me and propels me across the room, shoving me against the wall. Her fingers go to my belt buckle and before I know it, she's pulling my pants off. She drops to her knees as I step out of them. She looks up at me and grins.

"Don't move a muscle," she tells me.

"Okay, sweetheart." If she wants to have her way with me, I'm going to let her. I spread my arms wide. "Do what you want with me. I'm all yours."

CHAPTER FIFTEEN

Eleanor

AFTER I SLAPPED Rory without stopping to think what the consequences would be, there were only two things I could do. The first was to let him spank the shit out of me and then use my body to get himself off while leaving me hanging. That was not appealing. The second was to take charge of the situation and catch him off guard. That is working out better than I imagined it would.

As I drop to my knees in front of him, I can hardly believe Rory let me slam him up against the wall and practically tear his pants off him. Since he's rock hard, I guess he likes it when I'm more aggressive.

I take his cock into my mouth and breathe in his masculine scent. It's an intoxicating blend of his natural aroma and a deep, musky body wash. I suck experimentally, testing to see what he likes. When his moans tell me I got the pressure right, I cup his balls in the palm of my hand and caress him with my fingers.

I take Rory as deep as I can and then draw back. I repeat the action several times. He moves restlessly, dying to take over, but he holds himself back. That's a testament to the man's willpower. I bob my head a couple more times, letting his length slide over my lips, my tongue. Then I pull back and get to my feet.

Whipping my dress off over my head, I toss it to the floor. Then I remove my bra and panties. I leave my stockings on, because I know he likes that.

Rory watches me with something approaching awe as I step up to him. I wrap my arms around his neck and pull him in for a kiss.

It's not like when he claimed my mouth. This is soft, tender. I take it at my pace. My lips move against his. My tongue pushes into his mouth and I taste him. He puts his arms around my waist and pulls me closer. I moan as arousal thrums through my body.

Rory takes over now, deepening the kiss. He pours whatever anger and frustration he feels into it, robbing me of my breath. He walks me back to the bed and lowers me onto it.

Expecting him to take me hard and fast, I'm surprised when his kiss gentles. He climbs on top of me and positions himself between my widely spread legs. With great care, he slides into my sopping wet channel. The delicious stretch has my eyes rolling back in my head.

He kisses my neck, my shoulder, moving down to my breast. Taking the taut peak of my nipple into his mouth, he sucks hard. I writhe on the bed as the first wave of pleasure crashes over me.

Rory worships my body. His hands caress me, bringing each part of me to life. His lips suckle my breasts, making my insides tingle. He makes love to me in a way no man ever has before. We reach our peak together, and it's the most amazing thing I've ever experienced.

Rory pulls out of me, but he's nowhere near finished. He moves back and settles on his knees between my legs. Flashing me a cheeky grin, he lowers his head between my thighs.

He laps at me like he's feasting on a succulent fruit. His tongue teases my clitoris, drawing circles around it until I'm panting with desire. He pushes two fingers inside me and curls them to stroke that special spot that makes me squeal.

I lift my hips, looking for more. Perhaps I'm trying to get away. Who knows? I can't think straight when he's teasing me with his mouth like that.

Rory splays a hand across my stomach to hold me still as he continues to work me into a frenzy. My back arches and a scream tears from my throat as I come all over his hand. He doesn't give me time to recover, flipping me over and onto all fours. He pushes on my shoulders until I lower my head to the mattress. My butt is raised in the air, exposed.

"Stay like that," he tells me.

He leaves me for a moment, padding across the room to open a drawer. He returns a moment later with a large, flesh-colored dildo that's kind of obscene, and a bottle which I'm pretty sure contains lubricant.

"Do you know what I'm going to do to you, Eleanor?" he asks, a taunting note in his voice.

"No." I have my suspicions, but I want to hear him tell me what filthy things he plans to do to my body.

"I'm going to stuff this dildo in your pussy and you're going to hold it there while I fuck your ass."

At the very thought of it, I get even wetter.

"Spread your legs."

I do as I'm told, unable to resist that authoritative tone. Without warning, Rory shoves the dildo inside me. It's lucky I'm soaking wet from that last orgasm, because this thing is big. It's not as large as Rory's cock, of course, but still not for the faint-hearted.

"Now hold it there while I prepare your ass."

I grab the end of the sex toy and hold it in place as Rory dribbles some cool liquid on my ass. It tickles and I can't prevent a giggle escaping me. Rory slaps my ass and pain radiates out across my left butt cheek.

"Something funny, Mrs. Donovan?"

"No, sir."

"Hmm," he hums approvingly. I guess he likes that, but if he thinks I'm about to start calling him *sir*, he's going to be disappointed. That is not my thing.

I gasp as he smears the liquid around my tight hole and then slips two fingers inside me. It feels weird, foreign. I wouldn't call it painful, but it's definitely uncomfortable. With the dildo inside me as well, I feel impossibly full. I have no idea how his cock is going to fit.

He scissors his fingers apart, gently opening me up to him. He explores my rear channel for a moment and then pulls his fingers out. More lubricant drips down between my butt cheeks and Rory spreads it around. A moment later, the head of my cock breaches my virgin entrance for the first time.

He pushes in an inch or so before meeting resistance. My body tenses. It's too much. It hurts.

"It's okay, sweetheart," Rory assures me. "It'll get better. Trust me."

As he rubs my lower back soothingly, I realize I do trust him. Despite everything, I know he's not going to hurt me. I relax as much as I'm able and he slowly presses forward. He pulls back slightly and then pushes in once more, repeating the motion until he's fully seated inside me.

My breath comes out in short, desperate pants as I try to get used to the odd feeling. It's not just the stretch of my body that's strange to me. I'm also struggling to wrap my head around having my ass penetrated like this. It's dirty, forbidden. I can't breathe.

"It's okay," Rory says again. "Your ass was made for me to fuck."

His words spike my arousal. He thrusts into me, taking long, smooth strokes. There's pain, pleasure. It's awful and wonderful at the same time. I tremble beneath him.

"Fuck yourself," he orders me. "Slide that dildo in and out of your pretty little cunt."

His filthy command drives me wild. I move the silicone shaft out a few inches and push it back in. It takes a moment, but Rory and I establish a rhythm. As he withdraws, I shove the dildo into my body. I slide it out and he thrusts into me once more. We move in perfect harmony.

With my free hand, I grasp a handful of the bedsheets

and hold on for dear life. My womb clenches and my limbs shake as I'm hit by the most intense orgasm of my life.

I pull the toy out of my body and fling it away as I'm carried off on a wave of sensation. Blinding light flashes before my eyes and I cry out in ecstasy. My head spins and I collapse onto the bed, numb to the world around me.

When I come to my senses, I'm lying in Rory's arms, hot, sweaty and sticky between my legs. I'm a mess, but I've never been more satisfied.

"You okay, sweetheart?" Rory asks with concern.

"Yes, I am. Never better."

He strokes the side of my face. It's nice. It makes me sleepy.

"I want to make this work," he says. "I want us to start fresh. Will you give us a chance?"

"Yes." I snuggle into him. "I want that."

As I close my eyes, contentment washes over me. I know my days of resistance are over. I'm Rory's now and I think I like it.

ABOUT THE AUTHOR

Danielle Gillis loves to write about dominant men and feisty women. When she's not working on a novel, she likes to spend time with her husband in her hometown of Aberdeen, Scotland.

Sassa Daniels is a USA Today Bestselling Author of steamy romance in a variety of genres. Based in the Scottish Highlands, she lives with her husband and kids.

Also by Sassa Daniels And Danielle Gillis

The Donovans series

Chasing Liberty

By Sassa Daniels

Mafia Romance

Bystander

Penance

Defiance

Paranormal Romance

Claimed Mates Series